FELIX HARROW
INVESTIGATES

FELIX HARROW INVESTIGATES

PETER MCINTOSH

Table of Contents

Prologue

The Blackwood Estate stood as a symbol of grandeur and an architectural masterpiece. It had been home to the Blackwood family for generations which was a dynasty of wealth and influence that had shaped industries, supported charities, and whispered into the ears of world leaders.

At the centre of this empire was Richard Blackwood who was a man of immense power and charm, and who was well known for his strategic brilliance and philanthropic efforts. His wife, Margaret Blackwood, was the picture of grace, and a woman whose elegance was matched only by her sharp intellect. Together, they were the perfect couple and often envied by many but admired by all.

Richard's brother, George Blackwood, was equally respected although he preferred the quieter life of academia, and his pursuits more focused on history and philosophy rather than business. Yet he remained an essential figure in the family and a man whose wisdom and calm demeanour provided balance.

Then there was Eleanor Blackwood who was young, intelligent, and full of promise. At only nineteen years old she was already a star in the social circles of the elite, known for her kindness, wit, and striking beauty. With her chestnut brown hair, cascading in soft waves, and piercing blue eyes that seemed to see right through people, she was the kind of young woman who left an impression. Unlike many of her privileged peers, Eleanor was not only wealthy in material things but also in spirit, possessing an insatiable curiosity and an unbreakable moral compass.

The Blackwood family was untouchable or so it seemed. They had power, happiness, and an empire built on loyalty.

However, the Blackwoods were no ordinary rich family. Unlike the cold and detached aristocrats often found in the upper echelons of society, they were genuinely loved. Their wealth had been accumulated through generations of business acumen and investments in technology, real estate, and industries that shaped the world. But what truly set them apart was their dedication to using their influence for the greater good.

Margaret spearheaded numerous charities, mainly focusing on education and healthcare for underprivileged children. She had a presence that was impossible to ignore, and she always dressed immaculately, knowing the right thing to say and when to say it. She had been a guiding force in Eleanor's life teaching and reiterating to her that true wealth was measured not by money, but by the impact one left on the world.

Richard was a force in business and a man who could command a room with just his presence. He had built the

Blackwood empire into a global powerhouse, yet he remained deeply committed to his family. He ensured that Eleanor had the best education with the finest tutors and exposure to the most brilliant minds.

George, though less involved in the business world, was Eleanor's confidant. He saw in her a reflection of his own inquisitive mind, softly encouraging her love for literature, philosophy, and the mysteries of history. If Richard was the builder of the family's empire, and Margaret its heart, George was its quiet guardian and the one who saw the bigger picture.

Blackwood Estate was a place of joy, filled with music, laughter, and warmth. Parties hosted there were legendary, and it was not just for their extravagance, but for the genuine sense of community they fostered. Guests ranged from politicians to artists, scientists to activists, all mingling in the vast halls of the estate. And at the centre of it all was Eleanor.

As the only heir to the Blackwood fortune, it was not a surprise that Eleanor's future had always been a topic of speculation. Some believed she would follow in her father's footsteps and diligently take over the empire and lead it into a new age. Others thought she might dedicate her life to philanthropy, like her mother. A few even suspected she would rebel against her lineage altogether and start carving her own path.

But Eleanor herself was uncertain. She had never been interested in simply existing within the constraints of her privilege. She wanted to understand the world beyond Blackwood Estate and beyond the high society that she had been raised in. She had a fascination with history, with mysteries, and with the stories of people who filled the pages of history.

One day something unexpected happened without warning.

Eleanor was at the estate attending a dinner party with close family and friends, and she had been seen laughing, engaging in conversation, and looking as radiant as ever. There was nothing unusual about her demeanour, no sign of distress.

Suddenly, she was gone.

Her room was untouched, and her belongings still neatly arranged, her bed unslept in. There was no note, no sign of struggle and no indication of where she might have gone. The security cameras on the estate captured her going on a stroll alone, and was last seen exiting the estate, but it was not unusual for her to go for a walk on her own. She usually returned within the hour, but now it was as if she had simply vanished into thin air.

The Blackwood family was thrown into chaos. Richard used every resource at his disposal, hiring private investigators, enlisting the help of law enforcement, and even offering an astronomical reward for any information. Margaret was inconsolable, almost immediately retreating from the world as grief consumed her. George, the ever-calm presence, took a more methodical approach, pouring over Eleanor's journals, searching for clues in her writings.

But nothing led to her.

Rumours spread like wildfire. Some whispered that she had run away and that she was always desperate to escape her family's expectations. Others believed she had been taken, though by whom no one could say. A darker theory suggested that she had uncovered something she wasn't meant to, a secret buried deep within the Blackwood legacy.

Weeks turned into months, then years. The headlines faded, the world moved on, but the Blackwoods never did. The once happy and influential family became a shadow of itself. The estate, once filled with laughter and life, grew silent.

Margaret rarely left her room, with her health deteriorating from grief, and Richard, the man who had built an empire, now seemed hollow, his once-unshakable confidence replaced by an air of quiet despair. George, though composed on the surface, was never the same. He continued his search in private ever convinced that the answer was out there, waiting to be found.

But Eleanor was never seen again.

Despite her disappearance or maybe because of it, Eleanor remained an almost mythical figure. Her name was spoken in hushed tones at Blackwood Estate, her memory preserved in the hearts of those who had loved her. Some believed she was still alive, living under a new identity somewhere far away. Others were convinced that she had been lost to something darker, potentially to something beyond comprehension.

But one thing was certain was that her story was unfinished. And somewhere buried beneath secrets, and time, the truth about Eleanor Blackwood remained waiting to be discovered.

Within two years of Eleanor's disappearance both Richard and Margaret Blackwood were gone. Their deaths marked the tragic downfall of a family once considered untouchable and their story becoming the subject of hushed whispers and speculation for years to come.

Margaret had always been the pillar of grace and strength within the Blackwood family, but Eleanor's vanishing shattered something deep inside her. From the moment her daughter disappeared, she became consumed by a relentless sense of guilt, and an unshakable belief that she had failed her in some way.

At first, she tried to remain composed, feverishly throwing herself into the search efforts. She spent countless hours speaking with detectives, questioning staff, and reviewing every detail of Eleanor's final days at the estate. But the more she searched, the less she found, and the helplessness of it all began to eat away at her.

She replayed every moment leading up to Eleanor's disappearance in her mind, analysing her daughter's words, expressions, gestures, and desperately trying to pinpoint the signs she had missed. Had Eleanor been unhappy? Had she been trying to tell her something? Had she needed her mother in ways Margaret had failed to see?

As time passed and no answers came, Margaret withdrew from the world. She stopped attending charity events, stopped hosting dinners and stopped doing all the things that had once made her such a revered figure in society. Friends and family tried to console her, and all urged her to take care of herself, but she no longer seemed to care.

The once-vibrant woman, known for her elegance and quiet strength, started to wither away. Her health began to deteriorate rapidly before insomnia took hold, and she lost weight at an alarming rate. She would spend hours in Eleanor's room just sitting on her bed and running her fingers over her belongings as though trying to hold onto whatever traces remained of her daughter.

"She's out there," she would whisper to herself in the dead of night. "I should have known, and I should have done more."

Some said Margaret Blackwood died of a broken heart. Though the official cause of death was recorded as complications from an undiagnosed illness, but those who knew her believed otherwise. The pain of losing Eleanor had simply been too much and drained her of the will to go on. When she passed away, it was almost as if a part of Blackwood Estate died with her.

Richard Blackwood had built an empire but not even all his wealth and power could bring his daughter back. In the months following Eleanor's disappearance, he became a man possessed. He used every resource available, including private investigators, international agencies, and political connections, but no amount of money or influence uncovered the truth.

At first, Richard handled the crisis like he did everything else, which was with unwavering determination. He refused to entertain the idea that Eleanor might be gone forever, but as the months passed with no leads, the uncertainty began to crush him.

He became more volatile, more impatient. His famous charm and control began to unravel in public, his outbursts becoming more frequent and business associates whispered that he was losing his edge, that he had become distracted, and unpredictable. Some board members of his company even suggested that he step back for a while, but Richard refused.

Then Margaret died.

Her passing was the final blow. The woman who had been his partner, his equal, the love of his life was now gone. And in his heart, he knew what had truly taken her and it was not an illness, not a disease, but the unbearable weight of grief.

After her funeral, Richard stopped caring about appearances. He no longer bothered with the business and started leaving much of it in the hands of trusted advisors. He stopped socialising, stopped speaking to the press, and stopped playing the role of the indestructible titan of industry. He spent his days alone in his study, staring at photographs of his wife and daughter, drinking more than he ever had before.

One evening, just a few months after Margaret's death, he suffered a heart attack in his office at Blackwood Estate. The staff found him slumped over his desk with a framed picture of Eleanor and Margaret clutched in his hands.

The doctors called it stress induced from years of tension, and the heartbreak and exhaustion taking their toll. But those who knew him best believed it was something else.

Richard Blackwood had simply lost the will to fight.

With both Richard and Margaret gone, Blackwood Estate, which was once a place of joy and celebration, became a house of sorrow. The staff moved through the halls in silence, the air thick with the ghosts of what once was.

George Blackwood, Richard's brother, was left to manage what remained of the family's legacy. He took on the role reluctantly and not out of ambition but out of duty. Though he had always preferred a quieter life away from the business world, he could not bear to see everything his family had built crumble entirely.

In the wake of Richard and Margaret's deaths, George Blackwood found himself at the helm of the Blackwood fortune, but it was not out of ambition, but rather out of necessity. He had never been interested in wealth or power in the way his brother had been. While Richard had thrived in the world of business, turning the Blackwood name into one synonymous with success, George had always preferred a quieter life. But with Eleanor missing and both Richard and Margaret gone there was no one else left to protect the family's legacy.

George made a decisive choice and that was to step away from the world of high finance entirely. He had no desire to run the company his brother had built, nor did he wish to become entangled in the exhausting politics of boardrooms and markets. Instead, what he did was to sell off the business, liquidating the vast empire that Richard had worked so tirelessly to expand.

It was not a decision he made lightly, but it was the only practical one. Blackwood Enterprises was still valuable and by selling it at its peak, George ensured that the wealth his family had accumulated over generations would remain intact. He did not splurge or take unnecessary risks and instead he invested the proceeds into long-term, low-risk holdings, placing the family fortune into a structure that required little oversight and no active management.

The Blackwoods would never want for money but with the company gone their public influence faded. The name that had once carried weight in political and economic circles became more of a distant memory and a legacy rather than a living force, and George was perfectly fine with that.

While George was willing to let go of the business, there were some things he could not bring himself to part with, and that was Blackwood Estate and the family farm.

The estate had been the heart of the Blackwood family for generations. It was a place of history, of laughter, of life. The farm was a smaller but equally cherished property, and had been the family's retreat, a place where they had spent summers away from the pressures of society.

At first, George had told himself he would maintain both properties and keep them in pristine condition even if he had no intention of living there, but the years slipped away faster than he had anticipated. He had moved elsewhere purposely distancing himself from the past, while telling himself he would return to handle the upkeep soon.

But "soon" never came. Seasons changed, years passed, and before he knew it, the estate and farm had fallen into a state of abandonment. Without the constant care and attention that they required the buildings aged, the grounds became overgrown, and the once-beautiful halls began to gather dust. It was never his intention to let them deteriorate but maintaining them required more effort than he could justify, and the emotional toll of returning was too great.

Despite the neglect, George could not bring himself to sell.

Blackwood Estate was not just a house, it was the setting of his fondest memories. He could still hear the echoes of his childhood and of growing up with Richard, and of Eleanor as a little girl, running through the halls with boundless energy. He could still picture Margaret by the grand piano, playing softly in the evenings, and the scent of freshly cut roses from the estate gardens drifting through the open windows.

And then there was Eleanor always at the heart of it all, the one who had vanished without a trace.

Selling the estate felt like severing the last link to her and closing the door on the life they had all once shared. It was a piece of family history, a place that had stood for generations, far beyond Richard and Margaret, far beyond himself.

But while George could not let go, he also could not live there. The empty halls felt too heavy with loss. The once grand estate, filled with light and laughter, now seemed to him like a mausoleum to a family that no longer existed. He had no desire to roam those halls alone, constantly haunted by the ghosts of memories he could never recreate.

The same was true for the farm. It had been a sanctuary and a place where Eleanor had loved to ride horses, where summer picnics had once been filled with joy. Now, it was silent with nature slowly reclaiming what had been left untended.

Years passed, and the world around George moved on. Blackwood Estate remained untouched with its grandeur fading beneath ivy and dust, now a forgotten relic of another era. Some in the nearby town whispered about it, calling it cursed, a place where tragedy had left its mark too deeply to be erased. Others saw it as a mystery, a once-magnificent estate that now stood like a monument to something unfinished.

And yet, despite its state, George still could not part with it. He held onto it, perhaps irrationally, as if waiting for a reason, or maybe as if waiting for Eleanor.

Because deep down, even after all these years, he still hoped she might return.

And if she ever did, Blackwood Estate would be there, waiting for her.

The Beginning

Felix Harrow considered himself a smart man, a modern-day Sherlock trapped in the mundane world of freelance journalism. He often reminded himself that he was "a seeker of hidden truths", even though those truths often turned out to be disappointingly boring, obvious or a complete fabrication from his own mind. Still, he persevered.

On a particularly dreary Monday morning, Felix found himself staring at an envelope that had arrived through his letterbox. It was a thick cream coloured and slightly crumpled envelope, bearing the faint scent of old paper and something vaguely floral.

There was no return address. Just written in looping, elegant script: *"Investigator of Record."*

He hadn't given himself that title, not officially, but he was pleased someone out there had now recognised his genius.

With an air of self-importance, he slit the envelope open, and after pulling out a single sheet of folded paper his eyes skimmed over the words:

"You are in grave danger. They are watching. Do not

trust the obvious. The truth is never where you expect."

His pulse quickening as he reached the signature at the bottom.

Felix bolted upright in his chair and nearly knocked over the half-drunk cup of instant coffee on his desk. Did it say *Eleanor Blackwood?* The name didn't only ring a bell, it was more than that, it tolled like a cathedral chime. She had vanished under mysterious circumstances seven years ago, presumed dead after an extensive yet inconclusive investigation. The police had given up and the public had moved on, but Felix had been continuing with the investigation.

Here she was writing him a letter.

Felix leapt into action, or rather he fumbled around looking for his notebook and then his pen but realised he was still wearing his dressing gown. He rushed to his laptop with his fingers flying over the keyboard as he searched for any recent developments in the Blackwood case. Nothing. No one had reported any sightings, and no other cryptic messages had surfaced, until now.

And he was the recipient of this letter.

His mind whirred with possibilities. Had she faked her own death? Had she been held captive all this time? And what did she mean by they?

He needed to act fast and find where Eleanor Blackwood was when she wrote this letter.

Unfortunately for Felix, in his frantic excitement he ignored the many smudges on the signature where the ink had blurred to distort the name.

The letter had not really been signed by Eleanor Blackwood.

Felix decided to start at the last place Eleanor was seen, which was at the Blackwood family estate. The sprawling mansion had stood abandoned a few years after her disappearance and its once grand halls left to gather dust and silence, it was as though the house itself mourned her loss. Time had not been kind to the estate. Ivy coiled around the stone walls like a tightening grip, and windows stared out with dirty glass eyes. The heavy iron gates, which were once a proud entrance, now badly rusted.

Packing his notebook, a torch, and a half-eaten packet of biscuits which was the cornerstone of any serious investigation, Felix set off.

When he arrived, he hesitated. The air around the estate was thick and oppressive, charged with an eerie stillness that made his skin prickle. Even the birds seemed reluctant to break the silence. Steeling himself, he tested the gates but only for them to groan in protest, they were immovable. Climbing over was the only option.

Felix's attempt was anything but graceful as he hoisted himself up with difficulty, his foot slipping on the rusted bars. With all the elegance of a startled cat he tumbled over the other side and landed in an undignified heap on the overgrown gravel path. Cursing under his breath he dusted himself off, and straightened his jacket, as though there was someone around to witness his less than perfect entrance.

The house loomed before him with its dark windows hollow and empty, now just a relic of the past standing defiantly against time. The front door was locked so Felix continued moving around the outside of the house carefully, he crept along the perimeter, peering through grime coated windows hoping for a clue, or even a trace of movement, anything.

And then he saw it.

What looked like a candle that was flickering in an upstairs room.

His breath caught in his throat, The estate had been abandoned for about the last five years, and no one was supposed to be here.

Yet, the soft golden glow swayed against the darkness, a quiet defiance against the emptiness.

Felix's heart pounded against his ribs. Was it a squatter? Someone looking for shelter? Or had Eleanor... never left?

Felix's curiosity which was now a palpable force, started to tug him closer to the building. He stepped lightly with his boots that were muffled by the thick layer of leaves and dead ivy that had overtaken the estate's neglected grounds. The candlelight beckoned, still flickering like a silent invitation to uncover whatever secret lay hidden within those walls.

His pulse quickened as he reached the base of the house. The side windows now partially obscured by the tendrils of ivy, revealed only shadows within. But the room with the candle, he just had to see it up close. Slowly he made his way around the house, careful to avoid any broken glass or loose debris that might give him away.

When he reached the rear of the house he found a narrow service door, it was barely noticeable beneath the overgrowth. It was ajar, but just enough for a sliver of light to spill out into the gloom. His hand trembled slightly as he pushed the door open, with the hinges creaking in protest, and sending a shiver up his spine.

The scent of mildew and rotting wood hit him immediately, the oppressive smell of neglect and abandonment. The air was damp and heavy with five years of decay. Felix swallowed hard now trying to steady himself. The faint glow from the upstairs room still flickered in the distance, but now, it was closer, like a heartbeat drawing him deeper into the house.

Inside, the floorboards groaned under his weight, with each step echoing through the silence like a warning. Dust particles danced in the beams of light that were filtering through cracks in the walls. His eyes darted around now, scanning every shadow and every corner. He paused at the base of the staircase slowly taking a deep breath before beginning his ascent.

With each step the light above grew brighter, and the shadows darker. The hairs on the back of his neck stood on end as he reached the landing, his eyes searching desperately for any sign of movement or any hint that he wasn't alone. Then just as he rounded the corner, he saw it.

The room with the candle was just ahead with its door slightly ajar and a glow of light spilling out into the dark hallway. Felix felt his breath catch again in his throat.

Who would light a candle in a place like this?

He crept closer now with his heart hammering in his chest. Was it Eleanor? Had she returned, or had something else taken refuge in this forgotten home? As he reached for the door, he felt a cold gust of wind that seemed to rush past him sending a shiver through his body. He froze for a moment with his eyes widening, but his hand didn't hesitate. He pushed the door open inch by inch with his heart beating faster with each movement.

The room beyond was dimly lit, and the flickering candle was the only source of light now, casting long shadows across the walls. And there in the room, stood a figure.

The figure in the room was standing still, almost statuesque, with their back turned to Felix as they gazed out the window. The candlelight illuminated only a partial silhouette but was casting an elongated shadow across the floor. The light flickered casting eerie shadows that seemed to pulse with the very rhythm of the flame. Felix's breath hitched in his chest, he hadn't expected anyone to be here and certainly not in the shape of a figure that was so... still.

For a moment, Felix hesitated, with his instincts screaming at him to leave. But curiosity was now darker and stronger than any fear, which pushed him forward. He stepped into the room, and the floorboards creaked under his weight, but the figure didn't move. The air felt thick in the room and almost too still. There was a faint scent of something familiar, it was vanilla, mixed with the distinct musk of old paper.

Felix's eyes quickly scanned the room. It was sparse and almost barren. A threadbare armchair sat near the window, the only piece of furniture. The walls were lined with custom made bookshelves, but now their contents were largely abandoned with any remaining books cracked and yellowed with age. Dust clung to everything like a shroud. The faint smell of mildew still hung in the air, but there was something else, something peculiar, almost like an odd undercurrent, it was as though the room had been trapped in time.

He took another cautious step with his voice breaking the silence. "Excuse me, are you...?"

The figure turned, slowly and deliberate. Felix felt like he had forgotten how to breath as the candlelight revealed a face he hadn't seen in years. It was Eleanor.

But something was wrong, her face was pale, almost too pale, almost ghostly and with dark circles under her eyes as though she hadn't slept in weeks, perhaps months. Her hair which was usually neat and vibrant was now tangled and matted, hanging around her face in uneven strands. She wore an old, faded dress, with its fabric frayed at the edges, it was as though it had seen far better days.

She stared at him with her eyes wide, but not with recognition. They were vacant and hollow.

"Felix" she murmured, her voice distant and almost as if it wasn't truly hers.

Felix's heart skipped a beat. She was speaking his name, but the tone was wrong, and like she had forgotten how to say it properly. He took a step forward, with his hands shaking as he reached for her.

"Eleanor... What happened? Why are you here?" His voice cracked now desperate to bridge the gap between them.

She didn't respond immediately. Instead, she glanced over her shoulder at the window as if she were listening for something he couldn't hear. A shudder passed through her body, which jerked as if she had come back to herself. She blinked with a flicker of recognition flashing in her eyes, before it quickly vanished again, and was replaced by a look of confusion.

"I... I don't know" she whispered, her gaze shifting uneasily, avoiding his.

Felix felt a chill crawl down his spine. There was something strange about her, and about everything. The silence of the house, the strange flickering candle, and the way she looked at him as though he were both familiar and foreign at once.

Before he could ask more, Eleanor turned abruptly moving toward a shelf in the far corner. She paused for a moment and stared at a stack of old papers, before pulling something from underneath. Felix's heart raced as he recognised the object. It was a small and weathered box, a family heirloom, the one that had been rumoured to hold the key to the Blackwood family's secrets.

"What is that?" Felix asked, his voice now tense.

Eleanor's eyes flicked back to him, but the look she gave him was distant. "It's not mine. It's... for someone else."

Her hand clutched the box tightly, almost protectively as she backed away from him, her movement was erratic, as though she were being controlled by something he couldn't see.

Felix's stomach twisted with unease. This wasn't the Eleanor he remembered. There was something else, something dark and compelling anchored in this place, and it was keeping her tethered here. And the box? The secret it held might be the only way to understand what had happened to her.

But he didn't know if he could trust her anymore. Not with the way she was looking at him, like a stranger.

"Eleanor... you're not alone in here, are you?" Felix asked, his voice barely a whisper.

Her eyes flickered and for a moment, something like fear crossed her face, but she quickly hid it. The damage had been done. Felix knew deep down that whatever had been keeping her here and trapping her in this decaying estate, was far more than just the house itself.

Suddenly, Felix jerked awake, his breath coming in ragged gasps, his heart pounding in his chest. The room around him was dark, and the faint outlines of furniture blurred in the dim moonlight that was filtering through the curtains. The chill of the night air crept in through the open window, but it felt distant and unreal, as though he hadn't truly just awoken from a deep sleep at all.

His hands shook as he wiped his face, trying to push away the lingering sensation of Eleanor's cold, distant gaze. He could still hear her voice which was soft and broken echoing in his mind. "It's not mine... it's for someone else." The words felt like a riddle he couldn't solve. The box and the empty house, everything was still vivid and as though it had all really happened.

But that wasn't the case, it was just a dream.

He glanced at the clock on his bedside table with the numbers blinking in the darkness, 3:21 AM. The quiet ticking of an old clock was the only sound in the room which was now far too loud against the backdrop of the lingering unease.

Felix swung his legs out of bed and his feet touched the cold wooden floor. He stood up, now still trying to shake the heaviness that clung to him from the dream. A part of him didn't want to believe it had all been imaginary. The way Eleanor had looked at him and the way she had turned away from him, clutching that mysterious box, it had all felt too real.

He moved to the window carefully pushing aside the curtains to peer outside, as though expecting to see the

Blackwood estate just beyond the street with its decaying facade lit by a flickering candle. But all he saw was the darkened neighbourhood and the streetlights casting pools of orange light on the pavement.

A Clue with No Meaning

Felix shook his head hoping this would clear his thoughts. He could still feel the cold air of the house on his skin with the smell of dust and mildew that had clung to him. He rubbed his eyes and forced himself to focus on the here and now.

It was just a dream.

He sat back down on the edge of the bed with his mind racing. The images were already fading and slipping away like fog, but the emotion of fear and the confusion remained.

Was it his mind's way of telling him something? That box, Eleanor's strange behaviour, and the sense of being trapped within the estate, it all felt like a puzzle that demanded to be solved. But how could he solve it if it wasn't real?

The dream lingered now clawing at his thoughts. His fingers instinctively reached for the bedside table where his notebook and pen lay. He pulled it open and sketched quickly trying to capture the face of Eleanor from the dream, the way her eyes had looked at him, distant and hollow. Then almost without thinking, he drew the box, the one she had kept so tightly clutched in her hands.

Felix paused for a moment and stared at the drawing. It wasn't much, just rough lines with no detail. But it felt important. That box and that message, it was too vivid and too strange to ignore.

Was there a reason it had come to him now? Was there more to Eleanor's disappearance than he'd been told?

He ran his fingers through his hair trying to make sense of it. But for now, all he had was this one question echoing in his mind: If the dream wasn't real, why did it feel like a warning?

Felix couldn't shake the feeling that the dream hadn't been just a figment of his subconscious. It was as though his mind had unearthed something he couldn't quite grasp, and a thread of a mystery that tugged at him, but it was just out of reach. He'd spent the better part of the morning staring at his notes and the crude sketches. The box clutched tight in her hands was as if it were a symbol of something forgotten.

But the more he thought about it, the more elusive it became. What had it all meant? The cryptic message from the dream and Eleanor's strange words... It didn't fit and felt like a puzzle piece that belonged to an entirely different picture.

Sitting at his desk, Felix reached for his notebook again. He flipped through the pages filled with fragments of his real investigation into Eleanor's disappearance. But there were no new leads, and no new clues, just the same dead ends and no one had heard from her. No one knew where she had gone.

He ran a hand over his face, frustration building.

Then he froze.

Among the scribbles and scattered thoughts, he saw it: it was a sentence he had written days ago and something he hadn't thought about in the chaos of everything else. It was a note from a conversation with Eleanor's friend, Charlotte, just after the disappearance.

"The Blackwood family estate... there's something about that house. Something buried under layers of time and hidden right in front of us. But it's not what you think, it's not inside. It's in plain sight."

Felix had brushed it off at the time. Charlotte had been talking in riddles with her eyes darting around nervously as though she were afraid of saying too much. He'd never taken the words seriously, until now.

"Hidden right in front of us."

He scribbled the phrase down again while the words kept echoing in his mind, now louder than before.

Felix stood up abruptly and was suddenly filled with urgency. He grabbed his jacket, his notebook, and made his way to the door. If Charlotte's words meant anything, then the key wasn't buried in the estate. It was something *outside* of it. Something obvious and perhaps even overlooked.

He didn't know exactly what he was looking for but now he couldn't shake the feeling that it was out there waiting for him to see it.

The Blackwood estate was still where he had to go. It was the last place Eleanor had been seen after all. But now as he stared at the address in his notebook, Felix realised he'd been looking at the problem all wrong. He'd been searching for the wrong kind of clue entirely.

With a sudden clarity, he knew where he had to go.

The sun was starting to set as Felix made his way to the old Blackwood estate once more. This time however he wasn't heading directly to the front gates or the locked entrance. Instead, he circled around the back, keeping to the overgrown pathways that lined the property and avoiding the spots where the ground was too uneven or too noisy.

He had spent countless hours scouring the mansion's broken windows and the crumbling walls. It was falling apart so why hadn't he thought to look at the one place that was still, perhaps, most obvious?

The overgrown garden.

Felix made his way onto the estate and to a small, half, hidden door leading to a crumbling greenhouse at the far side of the property. The building was shrouded in vines and now almost entirely enveloped by the nature that it once took care of. The glass was shattered in several places now leaving the interior a shadowed mess of broken panes and jagged frames.

He paused at the door, staring at the debris piled up against it. Then with no hesitation he pushed through, very determined to find whatever Charlotte had been hinting at.

Inside, the air was thick with dampness and decay but the familiar smell of plants clinging to life through cracked soil was comforting. Felix walked carefully with each step cautious as he surveyed the interior. The floor was uneven and covered in dried leaves and the remnants of long forgotten plants. Yet despite the ruin, there was something oddly serene about the place. It was almost as if time had slowed here, and the walls of ivy were offering a sense of protection against the outside world.

As he walked deeper into the greenhouse something caught his eye. A small plaque was affixed to the far wall but obscured by a layer of moss and tangled roots. At first glance it appeared nothing more than a piece of forgotten ornamentation, or a relic of the house's once proud days.

But Felix felt a jolt of recognition. The plaque wasn't just decorative, it was engraved with a name.

"Eleanor Blackwood."

The name struck him like a lightning bolt. Why was Eleanor's name here like this and hidden away in this forgotten corner of the property? Felix stepped closer, his hand trembling slightly as he wiped away the grime that had accumulated over the years. Beneath the plaque was a year, and it was the same year Eleanor had vanished.

A sudden realisation dawned on him. This wasn't a forgotten piece of the estate, it was a memorial. But why had it been placed here and so far away from the main house in the neglected garden?

Felix stood still with his mind racing. He had found something, but not just a clue. This was a message and a clue that had been hidden in plain sight all along.

The discovery of Eleanor's name on a memorial hidden away in the overgrown garden felt important, but something still gnawed at him. This wasn't enough. It was as if there was a larger piece of the puzzle waiting just beyond reach.

And then, out of the corner of his eye, he saw it.

A flicker of light.

At first, he thought it might be the reflection of the setting sun or a trick of the fading light filtering through the overgrown trees, but no, there it was again. A steady and soft glow coming from one of the upper windows of the house, and it was the same place he'd seen the candlelight in his dream.

His heart skipped a beat.

Felix turned with his breath hitching as he stared at the house. The garden had obscured his view but now he could see it clearly in the upstairs window of the mansion, the window was faintly illuminated. The light seemed to sway, as though caught by a breeze. The same rhythm as in his dream.

No. This wasn't just a coincidence. It couldn't be.

Felix felt a wave of urgency wash over him with his legs moving before he'd fully processed his thoughts. He didn't know why, but the sight of the candlelight filled him with a strange sense of dread and determination. He had to get inside and had to know what was happening.

With a swift motion he turned and raced toward the back entrance of the house. His focus now remained solely on the house. The light, and it was real, it had to be.

He quickly approached the back door, the one he had previously found ajar during his earlier exploration. His pulse hammered in his throat as his hand reached for the cold brass knob. He pulled the door open with a reluctant creak, and he stepped inside, carefully moving through the narrow, dimly lit hallway with barely a sound.

It seemed so much like his dream with the same silence that hung in the air like a warning. But now with the glow from the upstairs room lighting his path, there was a new weight to the atmosphere.

The light from above beckoned him forward. Felix ascended the staircase with quick and deliberate steps, each footfall echoed in the house. As he neared the landing his hand hovered over the old door to the room with the flickering light.

He swallowed bravely gathering what little courage he had left. Then with a push, he opened the door.

And there it was, a candle flickering softly in the still air and casting its wavering light over the room. The shadows seemed to stretch unnaturally long across the floor, creeping toward him.

But unlike his dream, no one was standing there.

Felix's breath caught in his throat. The room was empty, save for a chair next to a small table by the window where the candle sat, the soft flame dancing in the silence. The window was open, just enough to let in the chill of the evening air, but there was no one in sight.

A cold dread came over him.

Someone had been here. Felix stepped further into the room now scanning every corner, but there was nothing, no trace of movement and no sign of life. Only the candle burning steadily, its glow bright in the dim room.

He turned back toward the door intending to leave when something suddenly caught his eye.

On the floor, just beside the window was a small scrap of paper.

Felix bent down to pick it up, his fingers were trembling slightly as he unfolded it.

The writing was hasty, and the ink smudged in places as though it had been written quickly and under duress. Felix's heart pounded in his chest as he read the words:

"It's too late. They're coming. They know you're here."

The message sent a shiver down his spine. The handwriting was unfamiliar, yet it felt urgent and desperate. Who had written this? And who were *they*?

Forgotten Souls

Felix's mind raced, his thoughts spiralling as he looked back at the candle. The light flickered once more and casted a shadow against the wall. It was as if the house itself were trying to tell him something and pushing him toward the truth, but not quite revealing it.

Suddenly he heard something, it was a faint creak, the sound of something heavy shifting. It came from the floorboards below. Felix froze with every instinct telling him to run, but his feet stayed rooted to the spot. His eyes darted to the door. Had someone entered the house after him? Or had *they* been waiting for him all along?

Felix unknowingly held his breath as he turned toward the door. The question was no longer just about Eleanor. It was about what was hidden here just beneath the surface, in plain sight. And now, it was becoming clear that whatever had been buried in this house and whatever had been waiting in the shadows, was finally beginning to reveal itself.

Felix stood frozen in the flickering candlelight, the scrap of paper still clenched tightly in his hand. His heart was pounding in his chest, but as the minutes ticked by and the initial fear that had gripped him began to ebb, it was replaced by a creeping sense of confusion. The room was silent, save for the occasional creak of the old house settling. No footsteps and no whispers in the dark. Just the quiet hum of the candle's flame.

It couldn't be. It couldn't be something *that* sinister. Could it?

Felix swallowed hard, staring at the note again. The message had seemed so urgent, so cryptic. *"They know you're here."*

But who were *they*? His mind spun with possibilities with each more unsettling than the last. He glanced around the room, his gaze scanning for any sign of movement. The window was still open with the breeze gently stirring the curtains, and the house around him felt more like a ghost than a home.

And then, just as the tension began to suffocate him, he heard another sound, it was a low muffled voice, distant but unmistakable.

Felix's pulse quickened again. He stood still, listening intently, trying to decipher the source of the voice. It was coming from somewhere downstairs, there was a murmur of conversation mixed with the sounds of movement.

For a moment he thought he imagined it, but the voices grew clearer and more distinct, as though someone, or some people, were speaking in the halls below. Felix hesitated for a moment now trying to process the sudden shift in the atmosphere. This house had been abandoned, or so he had believed. It was supposed to be a derelict shell that had been untouched for years.

But now...

Curiosity pushed him forward, and he cautiously stepped out of the room, moving toward the staircase. He kept his steps light making no sound, but the voices below became louder. His heart was still racing, but now it was more from confusion than fear. What was going on?

As he descended the stairs, he peered into the hallway, half expecting something, or someone to appear out of the shadows. But instead, he froze.

There, in the dimly lit entryway, a group of figures huddled together, sitting on the floor in a group. They were wrapped in layers of tattered clothing, their faces hidden in the low light. The scent of smoke, sweat and dampness hung in the air.

Felix blinked, his mind scrambling to make sense of the scene before him. The people, homeless perhaps, were muttering amongst themselves, laughing softly as they passed around a rusted tin can that seemed to serve as a pot. One of them looked up and Felix's breath caught.

The man's eyes were bloodshot, wild, and tired, but not hostile. He didn't seem surprised to see Felix standing there. Instead, he simply gave a slow nod, as if acknowledging his presence without caring too much.

"Bit late for visitors, isn't it?" the man said with a rough, gravelly voice.

Felix was stunned, still unable to process what was happening. He had been so sure, so convinced that the house was abandoned and that there was something sinister lurking within. But this... this was different.

"Who are you?" Felix finally managed to ask, his voice a little shaky.

The man shrugged nonchalantly. "We're just folks who found shelter. It's warm here. It's safe. We've been here a while."

Felix took a hesitant step forward, glancing at the others. There were three of them in total, two men and a woman, all of them with dishevelled hair and tired faces. They looked like they hadn't seen a proper bed or meal in days, perhaps weeks. And yet, there was a strange calmness to them, as though they had claimed this house as their own as a place of refuge amid the decay.

Felix's confusion deepened. This wasn't what he had expected at all. No dark figure, no grand mystery to uncover and no hidden family secrets. Just a few people who had found their way into the forsaken house and now making it their home in the shadows of the city.

He glanced around the room, taking in the makeshift living space they had created, a collection of old blankets, bags of belongings, and even a few books scattered on the floor.

Several candles strategically placed provided much needed light for the group now that the evening had arrived.

It was nothing like the eerie forgotten house he had imagined.

"Why here?" Felix asked, still trying to process everything. "Why the Blackwood estate? It's been empty for years..."

The woman sitting furthest away looked up at him, her face weary but not unkind. "No place else. People like us don't have a lot of options kid. The city doesn't want us, and this old house, well, it's better than the streets."

Felix stood there, his mind whirling. This wasn't what he had been expecting. No buried secrets, just a few homeless people trying to survive in a world that had long since forgotten them.

The woman caught his gaze and gave him a knowing look. "You came here looking for something, didn't you? Thought there was something going on in this house?"

Felix nodded, his face flushing with embarrassment. He had believed there was something dark, something twisted about the house. But now, seeing the people before him, hearing their simple, matter of fact explanation, it all felt so far removed from his suspicions.

"Sometimes, a house is just a house" the woman continued softly. "And sometimes, people make their own meanings out of the things they want to believe."

Felix felt her words sink in. The cryptic messages, the eerie feeling of the candlelight, it had all been his imagination running wild. He had let the mystery of the house consume him, and had let his fear and curiosity take him down a path that led to nothing more than a few souls seeking shelter.

But as he looked around, he realised that in the end, the truth was far simpler, and perhaps more tragic than he could have imagined.

The house had been empty for years and it wasn't filled with ghosts or secrets. It was filled with desperation and the will to survive, which had brought these people here.

Felix slowly turned to leave with his mind reeling. He hadn't found what he had expected, but in a strange way, he had found something more, something that made him reconsider his assumptions about the world, about mystery, and about what people are willing to do to survive.

Felix stepped out of the house and into the cold evening air, his breath fogging in the chill as he stood there processing everything that had happened. He felt a strange mix of relief and embarrassment. He leaned against the outer wall of the Blackwood estate, his mind replaying the events repeatedly.

Of course, the date on the plaque had made sense now. He hadn't connected the dots earlier, too caught up in the mystery of the place, the eerie candlelight, and the cryptic message in the room. The plaque bearing Eleanor's name and the date of her disappearance had felt like a clue he couldn't decipher. But now, he realised what it truly signified.

Eleanor had been a part of the family who once lived here, that wasn't a mystery. The real story had been lost to time, buried beneath layers of rumour, fear, and perhaps a touch of superstition. She surely wasn't part of some tragic secret locked within the walls of the estate.

And these people, the ones he had found huddled around the fire, the ones who had made this house their home, they weren't ghosts or anything dark or even mysterious. They were survivors, and they had settled here, where the echoes of the past seemed to linger. They had forged a life in the place that had once been a home to the family before.

Felix felt a pang of guilt as he thought of the way he had romanticised the house's mystery, how he had let his imagination run wild with possibilities. In the end it had just been a place that was now decaying, forgotten, and neglected, but not inherently sinister. And the plaque? It had been a memorial, yes, but perhaps just one of many in a family's long history. It didn't hold the key to a dark secret; it simply marked the loss of someone who had once lived here.

The figures he had met inside, the man with the wild eyes, the woman who had looked at him with understanding, had been living in the shadow of something far less romantic, less tragic, but perhaps more painful. They had been trying to escape the cold, the hunger, the harshness of the outside world, and they had found refuge in a place that others had abandoned.

Felix took a deep breath while looking up at the darkening sky. The house loomed behind him, quiet now, its windows dark, hollow eyes staring into the distance. At this distance, the candlelight was gone from view now. There were no more visible shadows dancing across the walls.

He had gone there looking for answers, chasing a mystery that wasn't there. He had been consumed by the idea of something greater, something hidden beneath the surface. But the truth had been right in front of him all along. The house, the plaque, the voices in the hall, none of it had been part of a grand puzzle. It was just a series of small, mundane things that had collided in a way he hadn't understood until now.

Felix let out a sigh, his shoulders sinking as he processed everything he thought he knew. He had expected answers, but all he had found were the quiet realities of life, the way people made do and the way history and people often blend in ways that aren't always obvious.

And now, all he could do was leave the house behind, knowing that the mystery he had chased had only led him to the most human of truths.

His steps slow but steady as he walked away from the Blackwood estate. The evening air bit at his skin but the chill felt oddly fitting. Sometimes, he thought, the cold was just a reminder that the world moves on, whether we're ready for it or not.

The fatal flaw

Felix continued down the path that led away from the forgotten house. As he moved, his mind continued to churn through everything he had just experienced. The homeless group, the plaque with Eleanor Blackwood's name and the unsettlingly familiar candlelight, all of it had shaken his certainty in a way he hadn't expected. His heart was still heavy with his assumptions and had begun to crack under the pressure.

But there was something else, something deeper still. The nagging sensation that he had missed something vital, that he had been so focused on solving the mystery, on finding answers where there were none, that he had ignored the one thing he should have seen all along.

And now, in the silence of his own thoughts, he saw it.

The letter. The one he had found in the empty room, the one that had felt so urgent and ominous, suddenly didn't seem as it had before. He had assumed it was somehow associated with Eleanor, that it was a desperate cry for help from someone trapped inside the walls of the house. It had seemed like the final clue and the key to unlocking the mystery of her disappearance.

But as he thought back to it now, Felix could see something clearly.

It must have been related to someone else entirely. And yet, Felix had been so convinced and so determined to make sense of everything, that he had latched onto the idea that it was related to Eleanor, maybe even her calling out from beyond the grave.

In his arrogance, he had thought he was the only one capable of solving the case. He had believed his instincts, and his sharp mind would lead him to the truth, that he could outwit the mystery and uncover the hidden past.

But now, Felix saw it with painful clarity: he had become the very thing he had always warned himself against. He had become blinded by his own assumptions, his own belief that he alone could untangle the threads of the Blackwood family history. He had made every decision based on what he wanted to believe, not on what was really in front of him.

The more he thought about it, the worse it got.

Each step he had taken, each turn he had made, had only led him further into a maze of half-truths, and dead ends. The cryptic messages? His own imagination, fuelled by his misguided determination. The eerie candlelight? Probably left in the room by one of the homeless people living in the house. Every misstep had been his own doing, he had overestimated himself, and in doing so, had failed to see the simple obvious truths that had been right under his nose.

Felix had told himself that he was different, that he could see things others couldn't, that he had the sharpness and the courage to uncover secrets that had been buried for years. He had been so certain of his abilities, and so sure that he was uniquely qualified to solve this case. But now, he was left with the stark realization that his self-assurance had been his fatal flaw.

He had believed that the key to solving the mystery was his alone to find. And in that belief, he had alienated himself from the very things that could have given him clarity, the truth, which had never needed to be uncovered through great feats of intellect or ingenuity. It was there all along, hiding in the mundane, the ordinary, and the overlooked.

Felix stopped walking, standing in the middle of the winding path as the realization dawned on him. The bitter taste of failure lingered in his mouth. His obsession had blinded him. His desire to solve the case, to tie up all the loose ends with the neatness of a detective novel, had led him to construct a mystery where none had existed. The people in the house hadn't been part of some larger, ominous plot. They were simply people, trying to survive in a world that had abandoned them. The plaque, the letter, it had all been symbols of something far simpler than he had wanted to admit.

Felix closed his eyes for a moment, the cool evening air filling his lungs as he exhaled slowly. He had to let go of his need to be right, his need to see himself as the only one capable of solving a mystery. Because, in the end all his decisions, and each step he had taken with such confidence, had only led him to a dead end.

The Blackwood estate wasn't a place of mystery. It wasn't hiding secrets or haunted by the past. It was just a house. And the only thing he had truly uncovered was his own arrogance.

Felix opened his eyes and began walking again, this time at a slower pace, with his head bowed in quiet reflection. There was no grand conclusion, no revelation that would explain everything. There was only the truth that sometimes the most complex mysteries are the ones we create for ourselves.

And Felix had created this one all on his own.

Felix stopped in his tracks as a thought struck him, a fresh wave of unease sweeping over him. The letter. The one that had arrived through his letterbox days ago. The letter that had started this latest goose chase.

Up until now, he had assumed it was a sign, a message from Eleanor Blackwood herself. The handwriting on the envelope, the words inside, all of it had felt deliberate, personal. The letter had been too specific, too pointed, to be anything other than a call for help. And it had been signed by her name, Eleanor Blackwood.

But now, in the cold evening air, Felix felt his chest tighten as a sudden realization began to take root. He had overlooked something so simple, so obvious, that it now felt impossible to ignore.

The signature.

He had never questioned it before, too caught up in the mystery of the message, too consumed by the idea that someone, somewhere, was reaching out. But now, as he thought back to it, something about that signature didn't sit right.

Felix could picture it clearly: the ink was smudged, not in a natural way, but as though the pen had been pressed down too hard in an attempt to force the letters onto the page. He could see it now, the way the final flourish, the "Blackwood" had not been written with the same care as the rest of the letter. It had been rushed. And as he recalled the name, it clicked, this wasn't Eleanor's handwriting at all.

Felix stood still, the letter's image flooding back into his mind. He hadn't noticed it in the moment, but now it was all too clear. The handwriting was erratic, uneven, and the signature? It wasn't her elegant cursive. It was a crude, jagged attempt to replicate it, but it had been signed by someone else.

His mind raced as he tried to make sense of it. Had someone forged Eleanor's name? Or was the letter truly a product of something darker? Whoever had sent it had gone to great lengths to create a false trail, to manipulate him into believing that Eleanor was reaching out from beyond the grave or wherever she was. But now, Felix realised with a sickening sense of clarity, the letter had been part of a web of deception.

The smudged signature wasn't a mistake. It was intentional and a sign of carelessness or perhaps panic. Someone had wanted him to believe in the story they were selling, to believe in the mystery of Eleanor's disappearance. But as Felix squinted in the growing dusk, trying to picture the signature in his mind, something began to emerge from the blur of ink.

It was someone else's. Someone he knew or at least should have known.

A flash of memory struck him. The signature was nothing like Eleanor's, but it was all too familiar.

It hit him like a punch in the gut.

Felix felt the blood drain from his face. His fingers began to tremble as the pieces fell into place. The letter hadn't been a message from Eleanor. It was from someone who had orchestrated the entire scenario. And they had been watching him, guiding him along a path that was nothing more than a distraction.

Felix's mind raced again, trying to make sense of everything. The house, the homeless people, the cryptic letter, all of it had been leading him to one conclusion: he had been played. He had let his own arrogance, his desire to be the one to crack this, completely blind him to the simple truth.

The letter had been a manipulation, a deliberate attempt to send him on a wild goose chase, and he had fallen for it. He had thought he was following the trail of Eleanor's disappearance, but instead, he had been following the trail orchestrated by someone else.

Felix clenched his fists, frustration bubbling up inside him. He had been so sure that he was the one who could solve this mystery, that his instincts would lead him to the truth. But now, all he saw was his own failure staring back at him.

In the dimly lit pub up the road, the clinking of glasses and the low murmur of conversation filled the air as a group of police officers sat around a large table, enjoying their drinks. The atmosphere was one of camaraderie and light, heartedness, a stark contrast to the tense mystery Felix had been so obsessed with.

"Bet he's tearing his hair out by now" one of the officers, a tall man with a thick beard, said with a chuckle, raising his pint of ale. "I can almost picture it, poor Felix, chasing after obscure clues and shadows like some detective in a bad novel."

Another officer, a woman with short, cropped hair, smirked as she leaned in closer to the table. "Oh, I'm sure he's well on his way to cracking the case wide open. *Not.*"

The group burst into laughter, the sound echoing through the pub. They had orchestrated the entire charade with a level of precision and amusement. The cryptic letter they had sent to Felix hadn't just been a prank, it had been part of a much larger plan. They had watched Felix's every move, expecting him to stumble into their trap. And they had been right.

"The poor guy has probably spent hours trying to figure out that stupid letter" said a younger officer, his grin wide and playful. "All that talk about 'Eleanor Blackwood' - he probably thinks he's about to uncover some long-lost family secret. Meanwhile, we've been laughing our heads off."

"Do you think he's figured out that it was us?" the tall officer asked, eyes gleaming with mischief.

"No chance" replied the woman, her tone dripping with amusement. "Felix is so wrapped up in his own head, he wouldn't spot the obvious if it jumped up and bit him. He's too busy trying to outsmart himself."

The group exchanged knowing glances, and a ripple of laughter passed between them again.

"Bet he's already off at the Blackwood estate, poking around in the dark, convinced there's some hidden clue in the walls" the tall officer continued, wiping a tear from his eye. "Can't wait to see him back here, all sweaty and red, faced, trying to explain how he missed the big *obvious* clue."

The younger officer, still laughing, shook his head. "I'm just waiting for him to get really deep into it, you know? Get so wrapped up in solving this thing that he starts seeing shadows where there aren't any. It'll be a great show."

They all took another sip of their drinks, their laughter subsiding into chuckles and smirks. The officers revelled in the ease of the game they were playing, enjoying every moment of their small triumph over the "detective" they had come to view as a bit of a joke.

"He's going to be so far off track" said the woman with a gleam in her eye. "And when he does realise it was us all along, that's going to be the best part. The look on his face!"

The officers fell into a comfortable silence for a moment, the hum of the pub's conversation and the clinking of glasses filling the space around them. They all knew how it would play out. Felix would chase after unverified clues and signs, digging deeper and deeper into a case that had never really been a case at all. They had fed him just enough to keep him on the trail, and he would bite. They were certain of it. It was all part of their game. They couldn't wait to see how far he would go, and just how spectacularly he would fall.

It was only a matter of time before Felix came crashing back to reality. And when he did, they'd be there, waiting, to see the final punchline of the whole thing.

Red Hat Café

The Red Hat Café wasn't much to look at from the outside. Its red awning, weathered and peeling, hung crookedly above the entrance, and the windows needed cleaning. The small café was tucked between two larger buildings, a forgotten corner of the town where time seemed to slow down. The faint smell of burnt coffee and stale pastries lingered in the air, but there was something oddly comforting about it.

Felix stood outside for a moment, adjusting the collar of his coat as the wind bit into him. He wasn't sure why he had come here and why he had chosen this café, but the intuition that had guided him through the twists of the mystery had led him to this very spot. His gut told him he would find answers here. He just couldn't shake the feeling that something was about to change.

Pushing open the door, Felix stepped inside, the warmth of the café hitting him instantly. The low murmur of voices filled the space, blending with the soft clink of cups and saucers. He scanned the room, spotting a man sitting alone at a corner table, hunched over a coffee but also staring at the door as though he had been waiting for him.

Felix's heart skipped a beat.

This was the meeting. The one he hadn't expected but had known was coming.

The man raised his eyes when Felix entered and motioned to the empty chair across from him. Felix hesitated for a moment, then moved towards the table with his curiosity piqued. There was a weight in the air, something heavy and unspoken and as if the walls of the café were holding their breath.

"You're late" the man said, his voice low, but friendly. He had a sharp and angular face with a shadow of stubble, his eyes cold and calculating.

Felix took a seat, his eyes narrowing. "I wasn't aware we were on a schedule."

The man smirked, a small, almost imperceptible quirk of his lips. "Time is irrelevant. What matters is that you've come and that you're still following the trail."

Felix leaned forward, studying the man. "I don't know who you are, but you're the one who sent the letter, aren't you?"

The man didn't answer immediately, just took another sip of his coffee, his eyes never leaving Felix's face. The silence stretched for a moment before he spoke again.

"It's not about the letter. It's about the bigger picture" the man said, his tone taking on a more serious edge. "You've been chasing something that doesn't exist. A ghost. And all this time, you've been too blinded to see the truth."

Felix's pulse quickened. Was this the moment when everything would finally make sense? The pieces of the puzzle he had been assembling in the dark might finally fit together.

"What truth?" Felix asked, leaning in. "What exactly are you trying to tell me?"

The man looked over his shoulder briefly, then lowered his voice, leaning in as well. "The Blackwood estate. Eleanor Blackwood. None of it is what you think. You're asking all the wrong questions, Felix. You're wasting your time on the past, chasing a family that's been dead for years. What you need to focus on is now. The people who are alive, the ones who are still in control."

Felix's mind whirled. This wasn't what he had expected at all. The man was offering no details, only more riddles and half answers. Yet, there was something about his words that felt dangerously close to the truth. He had been chasing shadows in the Blackwood estate, but this, this was a new direction, a new path.

"You're telling me to stop looking for Eleanor" Felix said slowly "but why? Why am I chasing the wrong things? What's really going on?"

The man's lips twisted into a tight smile. "Because you're too wrapped up in the past. You're digging in the wrong places, focusing on a tragedy that never even happened. Eleanor Blackwood wasn't the key to this mystery, Felix. She was just a pawn. The truth has been staring you in the face all along."

Felix felt a cold shiver run down his spine. He had always suspected that something was off, that the case wasn't as simple as it appeared. But now the man's cryptic words were pushing him further into a tangled web he didn't yet understand.

"What do you mean?" Felix pressed, though a voice inside him warned that he was about to fall into a trap.

"Look at the people around you" the man said, gesturing vaguely toward the other patrons in the café, who seemed to be too preoccupied with their own lives to notice the conversation unfolding. "Look at the ones who have always been there, who've shaped everything you've seen. The letter you received, it wasn't from Eleanor. It was never her. But you'll find out who it really came from soon enough. Don't waste any more time on things that don't matter."

Felix's heart hammered in his chest. The words felt like a puzzle in themselves, but the more he heard, the less sense they made. He was being told to stop looking for the truth, to abandon everything he had worked for, but the man wasn't offering anything in return, just more ambiguity.

Suddenly, Felix saw the man's eyes flicker toward the window, then back to him. The moment was fleeting, but it was enough to make Felix pause.

"You're not going to tell me who you are, are you?" Felix asked, his voice suddenly sharp.

The man gave a casual shrug. "Does it really matter? I'm not the answer. You are, Felix. You've been chasing leads and clues, but I'll tell you this, there are people who have been using you. You've been nothing but a pawn in a game and you're too far in to back out now."

The warning hung in the air like a weight. Felix was about to ask him more, but the man stood up abruptly, pulling on his coat.

"You'll figure it out and you'll see the truth eventually. But it's too late now. Good luck."

Without another word, the man stood up and left the café, leaving Felix to sit alone at the table.

Felix stared at the door, he had come here looking for answers, but all he had found was more confusion and more lies wrapped in a facade of truth. And now, with the man gone, Felix knew one thing for sure: whatever game had been played with him had only just begun.

He stood up slowly, slipping his coat on. The patrons of the café none the wiser to the dangerous game that had just unfolded at the corner table.

But Felix knew that things were about to get far more complicated.

And the truth? It was still just out of reach.

Felix had built a career around exposing the hidden truths, particularly when it came to people of power. As an investigative journalist, his primary mission was to shed light on corruption, deceit, and abuse, whether it was in government, corporations, or other powerful institutions. His job wasn't to play the role of detective, he didn't chase criminals or make arrests. Instead, he dug deep into the stories that others overlooked, the ones that were buried beneath layers of misinformation or public silence.

While he had sometimes found himself solving pieces of criminal cases along the way, that was never his goal. His work wasn't about catching criminals; it was about uncovering the systems and individuals behind the wrongdoing. The law enforcement agencies would take it from there. Felix saw himself as a catalyst for investigation and the spark that would ignite the machinery of justice, not the hand that wielded it. He knew that once the truth was out in the open, the wheels of the law would take over, and the appropriate action would follow.

But in his mind, the prosecution wasn't the journalist's job. Journalists like him were there to ask the hard questions, expose the facts, and get the story out. The law was supposed to handle the consequences.

Felix liked to think of himself as the "detective of the written word." It wasn't a title anyone had given him, but one he'd claimed for himself, and he wore it with a sense of pride. He saw his work as an investigator in the world of written language, the ability to uncover hidden meanings, the subtle hints in a phrase, the unsaid truths between the lines. Just as a detective followed physical clues to solve a case, Felix followed the clues in the words people wrote, whether in public records, private documents, or in the very fabric of stories that people tried to hide.

To Felix, every piece of writing was a mystery waiting to be solved. He would pick apart statements, reports, letters, and contracts with the meticulousness of a seasoned detective. The words could speak volumes if you knew how to read between them. It was all about unearthing the intentions, the motivations, and the narratives people wanted to conceal.

His colleagues often joked about his self-proclaimed title, but Felix had always believed that the written word could be just as revealing as a footprint, or a fingerprint left behind at a crime scene. That's why he was able to dig up the truths that others might have missed.

Even though Felix prided himself on being the "detective of the written word" he wasn't one to shy away from getting his hands dirty when the situation demanded it. The written word could reveal a lot, but there were times when a deeper, more personal investigation was necessary to get the full picture. He knew the value of being physically present, of speaking to people face to face, or walking the streets and buildings that were part of the story.

If his research pointed him to a location, he'd go. If someone's words didn't match their actions, he would confront them. While he relied on documents, reports, and correspondence to uncover the truth, Felix wasn't afraid to dig into the physical world when the written clues led him there. Whether it meant visiting a crime scene, speaking to witnesses, or even snooping around places others wouldn't dare, Felix understood that his role wasn't limited to what was on the page. Sometimes the full picture required him to get out there, gather physical evidence, and follow leads wherever they took him.

His investigative methods were a blend of keen observation, careful research, and a willingness to take risks. He didn't just uncover the truth with words, he chased it wherever it hid.

Despite his sharp skills and keen intuition, Felix wasn't immune to chasing clues that ultimately led him in circles. His drive to uncover the truth could sometimes cloud his judgment, pushing him to follow threads that seemed promising at first, only to reveal nothing but dead ends. It was frustrating but inevitable. The world of investigations wasn't a neat, linear path; it was full of misdirection's, half-truths, and false leads that could easily lead someone like Felix to waste time and energy.

Sometimes, the more he dug, the more convoluted the case became. He would follow a lead that seemed to connect to something larger, only to find it had no real relevance. The written clues he relied on would sometimes unravel into a string of contradictory statements, pulling him in different directions. There were times when he would revisit a location or a person, convinced he had missed something, only to find himself retracing the same steps, no closer to the truth than before.

But Felix wasn't the type to give up easily. Even when the leads seemed to go nowhere, he would keep searching, determined that the next clue would be the one to crack the case wide open. His persistence was both a strength and a flaw, because sometimes he ended up chasing clues, ideas, or theories that weren't grounded in reality. It was in those moments that he had to take a step back and remind himself that not every clue was meant to be solved immediately, and not every trail was worth pursuing.

Allies

Felix had learned long ago that allies came in all forms. Some were dependable, others were unpredictable. But sometimes, the line between friend and foe blurred, and the ones he thought were most useful turned out to be the ones who were least prepared for the mess he was getting them into.

He had met Sofia at a small gathering of local journalists a few months before, and they'd struck up an easy conversation about their mutual frustrations with certain unsolved cases in the region. She was bright, inquisitive, and more than willing to lend a hand when needed. To Felix, she seemed like the perfect kind of ally: someone eager to make a difference and willing to help uncover the truth.

But as the case surrounding Eleanor Blackwood deepened, Felix found himself calling on Sofia more and more. Not because he trusted her expertise, she was still green when it came to high stakes investigative work, but because she seemed like someone who could at least keep up with his quick thinking and provide fresh eyes on a situation that had begun to feel like a maze.

The moment he asked her to come along on his latest search, he had no idea that his reliance on her would end up being one of the most chaotic, yet oddly helpful, decisions of the investigation.

It happened when Felix was digging into the local archives, trying to piece together the Blackwood family's financial history. The documents were thick, dense, and mostly irrelevant, but there was something in the margins, a note in the handwriting of someone from years ago that had caught his attention. It was a lead that seemed too vague to chase by himself, but Sofia was there, sitting across from him, scanning through old records with the sort of casual dedication Felix could never quite match.

"Do you think this is important?" Sofia asked, holding up an old photograph she'd found, one that showed an unknown person standing in front of the Blackwood Estate. She passed it to Felix, who took a quick glance before setting it aside.

"Maybe, I will take a closer look" Felix muttered, his mind still wrapped around the note he'd seen in the margins of the financial records.

Sofia shrugged, going back to her task. "Just thought it looked like something worth holding onto."

Felix didn't even register the photo again until later, when the pieces of the puzzle started to align in ways he hadn't expected. It wasn't the photo itself that held the clue, but something Sofia had inadvertently said while tossing it aside. She mentioned off hand that the person in the photo looked familiar, but she couldn't place where she'd seen the face before.

That one little remark, a comment she had made without thinking, would set Felix off in a new direction, one he had never considered.

He dug into the local archives again, this time focusing on connections he hadn't thought to explore. He pulled up old case files, looking into missing persons, local scandals, and any minor figures who could have slipped under the radar. It was only when he started cross referencing names that the connection hit him. The figure in the photo had once been a suspect in a completely unrelated case, one that had been closed years ago. The resemblance was startling, and the implications... well, they were too significant to ignore.

Sofia, completely unaware of the magnitude of her off hand observation, had accidentally helped Felix uncover something that might have been key to solving the case. But the more he thought about it, the more he realised that she had no idea what was really happening, what he was really digging into.

Felix couldn't blame her. Sofia had no way of understanding the complexity of the situation. She was just a well-meaning journalist caught up in something far bigger than she had ever intended. She wasn't trained for this kind of investigation. She didn't know how deep the rabbit hole went. And yet, it was her casual comment, her off the cuff remark that had pushed Felix toward a new revelation.

Felix found himself staring at the photograph again, the puzzle slowly coming together. He'd thought Sofia was just a sidekick in this case, someone to run errands or brainstorm ideas. Instead, she'd unknowingly pushed him to a piece of the puzzle that had been hidden in plain sight all along. He would need to dig even deeper, and perhaps now he had the key to something far more dangerous than he had anticipated.

As Felix stood up and turned to Sofia, preparing to fill her in on the new development, he realised one thing: sometimes the most unexpected allies were the ones who didn't know they were helping at all.

And sometimes, even the most well-meaning allies could unwittingly become the wild cards that shifted everything.

The person shown in the photo was a suspect in a case that had been closed years ago was known as "The Holloway Vanishing." It was a case that had stirred up plenty of speculation at the time but had ultimately faded from public memory after no concrete answers had emerged.

Five years ago, a local historian named Victor Holloway had disappeared under unusual circumstances. He had been researching the history of old estates in the region, with a particular focus on aristocratic families. His last known project had been a deep dive into the Blackwood family.

Victor had been seen leaving his small rented flat one evening, carrying a leather satchel filled with notes, documents, and an old journal he had acquired through unknown means. He told his colleague at the local history society that he was onto something "big", something that would "rewrite the story of the Blackwood name."

He was never seen again.

At first, his disappearance was treated as a simple missing persons case, but when authorities searched his flat, they found it ransacked, as though someone had gone through his belongings with a fine-toothed comb and taking whatever was of value. His notes were missing, his satchel was never recovered, and his personal effects were left untouched, suggesting that the disappearance wasn't a robbery gone wrong.

The only clue left behind was a single torn photograph, showing a figure standing in front of the Blackwood estate. The face was slightly obscured, whether by accident or design was never determined. The authorities concluded that Victor had likely run off on his own accord, possibly after getting too wrapped up in his research and losing his grip on reality. The case was officially closed due to lack of evidence.

Felix, of course, had never bought into that explanation.

Now, years later, Sofia had unknowingly stumbled upon the same photograph from the Holloway case, this time buried deep in the local archives, hidden among old estate records. Seeing it again, Felix felt a jolt of recognition. He remembered coming across that image when he had first read about Victor's disappearance, but back then, it had been nothing more than a strange footnote in an unsolved case.

But now... now it was different.

If the same obscured figure was appearing in both Victor Holloway's research and Eleanor Blackwood's disappearance, then there was something connecting the two cases.

Something, or someone, had made Victor vanish.

And if Felix kept digging, he had a feeling he might find out why.

Felix stared at the photograph in his hands, the one Sofia had unknowingly unearthed. Victor Holloway's disappearance. A case long thought to be unsolved. A case that might have been tied to Eleanor Blackwood.

But something about it wasn't adding up.

The Holloway Vanishing had been filed away as an unsolved mystery, yet there was no clear reason why it had been abandoned so quickly. Felix had always assumed it was due to lack of evidence. But as he dug deeper, cross, referencing old police reports, archived newspaper articles, and some notes he had scrawled down years ago, he stumbled upon something that stopped him cold.

Victor Holloway had been found.

Not dead. Not abducted. He was just living with his mother in a quiet seaside town.

Felix blinked at the report in front of him, feeling like the floor had just dropped out from under him.

According to police records, Victor had reappeared months after his so called disappearance. There had been a break in at his flat, which had rattled him enough that he had simply packed his things and left. No cryptic clues, no dark conspiracy, he was just a man who wanted to be left alone.

And yet, no one had ever corrected the public record. The mystery of "The Holloway Vanishing" had remained exactly that, a mystery.

Felix ran a hand down his face, feeling equal parts frustrated and ridiculous.

How had he missed this?

He had thought Victor's case was a tangled web of secrets. He had theorised about cover ups, assumed something sinister had taken place, followed false leads. And yet, the truth had been out there the whole time.

In fact, when he casually brought it up at a local pub later that evening, expecting to drop a bombshell revelation, the response he got was laughter.

"Oh, you didn't know?" one of the regulars chuckled, shaking his head. "Yeah, Victor's fine. He just couldn't deal with the hustle and bustle anymore. Lives with his mum now, nice woman."

Another journalist, one of Felix's acquaintances, raised an eyebrow at him. "I thought everyone knew that?"

Felix exhaled sharply, running a hand through his hair. Of course, he had spent so much time convinced he was chasing something big, when it was common knowledge to everyone but him.

Still, as much as it stung his pride, he wasn't ready to drop it just yet. Because even though Victor's disappearance wasn't a disappearance, there was still one question that nagged at Felix.

What had he been so scared of that he left his entire life behind?

And why had his research led him to the same photograph.

The wrong suspect

There was a time when Felix was seen as a rising star in investigative journalism, sharp, relentless, and always chasing the next big revelation. He had a knack for uncovering corruption, but his biggest problem was that often no one seemed to care about the things he exposed. He had written a hard-hitting piece about a local mayor misusing public funds, this was buried on page seven. He had revealed a businessman's shady offshore accounts, and this was met with nothing but a shrug from the public.

But then came the scandal that never was.

Felix had been tipped off about a famous chef, Gregory Langston, a culinary genius with an empire of Michelin star restaurants. A source, who in hindsight, was both unreliable and slightly intoxicated, had fed Felix an outrageous claim. Apparently, Langston was running an underground fight club beneath one of his high-end establishments. The source spoke of bruised employees, secret high stakes illegal gambling, and a basement where chefs allegedly settled disputes with their fists.

Felix, desperate for a story that would finally put his name on the map, went all in.

He published a scathing exposé, detailing the alleged "Gourmet Fighting" complete with anonymous testimonies and what he thought was damning circumstantial evidence. The public reaction was immediate, headlines exploded, social media went wild, and Langston's reputation teetered on the edge.

Then, reality hit.

The so, called "Gourmet Fighting" turned out to be a free cooking programme for troubled youth, which was run in the evenings out of the restaurant's basement kitchen.

Langston, to his credit, didn't sue. He didn't have to. Instead, he invited Felix to a televised press event, where he personally handed him a ladle and said: "Since you seem so interested in my work, perhaps you'd like to learn how to actually investigate before you write."

The humiliation was legendary.

Felix's credibility took a nosedive. Editors stopped taking his pitches seriously. His name became shorthand in the industry for "sensationalist disaster."

And now, here he was, years later, desperate for a case that would redeem him. A case that would prove he wasn't just the guy who once mistook a youth outreach programme for an illegal fight ring.

The problem? He kept getting everything completely wrong.

Every lead he chased turned into a dead end. Every shocking discovery was either old news, misunderstood, or a prank at his expense. He had convinced himself that Victor Holloway had vanished into thin air, except he hadn't. He had thought the police were covering up a deep conspiracy, but they were just laughing at him over pints.

Felix was determined to break a case that would restore his reputation.

But if history was any indication, he was far more likely to trip over his own mistakes before he ever got close to the truth.

Felix had spent weeks chasing the tangled mess of the Eleanor Blackwood case. False leads, dead ends, police pranks, he had endured it all. But now, finally, he had something.

Something real.

He had been following up on an old name connected to the Blackwood estate, a former groundskeeper, Bernard "Bernie" Kessler. The man had worked for the Blackwood family for over thirty years, right up until Eleanor's disappearance. And then, without warning, he had left town, slipping into obscurity.

Felix was convinced that Bernie was hiding something and had tracked him to a modest little house on the edge of a neighbouring town. Under the cover of darkness, because naturally Felix had poor impulse control, he found his way into Bernie's shed.

And that's when he saw it.

The box.

It was an old, battered wooden chest, tucked away beneath a workbench. The second Felix pried it open, he felt his pulse skyrocket. Inside, wrapped in layers of cloth, was a bloodstained silk glove. Elegant, delicate, fitting of someone like Eleanor Blackwood.

Felix's heart hammered. He had found it. Proof. Evidence. The missing piece.

His hands trembled as he took photos, his mind already racing ahead. Headlines. Justice. Redemption.

But then, the shed door swung open.

Bernie Kessler, a wiry old man with permanently furrowed brows, stared at him in absolute confusion.

"What the hell are you doing in my shed?"

Felix, still holding the glove, barely managed a response. "Uh, investigative journalism?"

Bernie sighed, walked over, and snatched the glove out of Felix's hand.

"That's my wife's. From our wedding day. She cut her hand on some broken glass, bled all over it. I kept it because I'm sentimental, not because of anything sinister. Get out of here before I call the police!"

Felix felt all the air leave his lungs.

For a long moment, the two men just stared at each other.

Then Bernie muttered "Idiot" and walked out of the shed, leaving Felix standing there, holding his camera, his once, brilliant discovery now just an awkward misunderstanding.

Felix left Bernie Kessler's house feeling like an absolute fool. Again.

He had stormed in, expecting to find a missing piece of the puzzle, only to end up accusing a retired groundskeeper. Fantastic work, truly. If he kept up this level of investigative excellence, he'd soon be back to writing articles about dodgy pub menus.

The cold night air did nothing to clear his frustration as he trudged down the empty street. He was just about to reach his car when something caught his eye, a shape, half hidden in the shadows near a row of bins.

A person.

Felix froze. The figure was sprawled awkwardly against a low brick wall, one arm outstretched, their head tilted at an unnatural angle. Not moving.

Every instinct in Felix's body screamed dead body.

His heart rate spiked as he cautiously stepped forward. "Hey..." he called out, his voice hesitant. No response, no movement.

Oh, bloody hell. This was it. He'd spent weeks chasing after what he thought were clues, and now, out of nowhere, he had found a corpse.

He swallowed hard and pulled out his phone with shaky fingers, ready to call the police, until he hesitated. Something wasn't right. The angle of the body, the slight rise and fall of their chest,

Wait, breathing?

Felix stepped closer, holding his phone's torch up to their face. A man, maybe mid-40s, unshaven, wearing a tatty old coat. A faint groan escaped his lips.

Not dead, unconscious.

Felix exhaled so sharply he almost laughed. He had gone from 'accusing an innocent man of murder' to 'stumbling across what he thought was a body, but was just an unconscious guy' all in the span of ten minutes. His reputation as an investigator was reaching groundbreaking levels of incompetence.

Still, he couldn't just leave the man here. "Mate" Felix said, nudging his shoulder lightly. "Are you ok?"

Another groan. A muttered curse. A slow, sluggish blink as the man's eyes flickered open.

"Right" Felix said, mostly to himself. "Not a dead body. That's... good. I think."

The man squinted at him, then at his surroundings, looking vaguely disoriented. "Who the hell are you?" he muttered.

Felix considered the question for a second before sighing.

The man grunted, rubbed his eyes, and then, as if it was entirely normal to wake up half in a gutter with a stranger standing over you, just shrugged and went back to sleep.

Felix stared. "Yeah, okay. You do that."

He turned away, shaking his head. Maybe it was time to rethink his approach to investigative journalism.

Felix was, by all accounts, having a terrible time with the Blackwood case. Every lead turned into a joke at his expense, every breakthrough crumbled in his hands, and at this rate, he was starting to wonder if he should just retire and open a sandwich shop instead.

But then, entirely by accident, he did something brilliant.

It happened in the early hours of the morning, when Felix, still buzzing from his latest failure, stumbled into a grimy café in desperate need of caffeine and a reason to keep going. He was halfway through his coffee, black, no sugar, because self-loathing tasted better that way, when he overheard a conversation at the next table.

Two men, speaking in low voices. Too low.

Felix didn't mean to eavesdrop, but they were whispering with the urgency of people who didn't want to be heard, which, naturally, made Felix listen harder.

"...all over the papers soon" one muttered.

"Not if we shut it down first" the other said.

Felix, who had spent far too much of his life chasing badly disguised conspiracies, leaned in slightly, pretending to be extremely interested in stirring his coffee.

The men spoke in vague terms, shipments, accounts "adjusting" numbers, but Felix's brain, trained for corruption even if it rarely found any, started piecing it together. Financial fraud. Maybe even embezzlement.

Then came the golden line.

"Walker's got everything on his laptop" one of them grumbled. "If that gets out, we're finished."

Walker. Felix knew that name. David Walker, finance director for a mid-sized energy firm that had been under quiet investigation for dodgy dealings. Felix had written about them years ago, before his credibility took a nosedive. No one had cared.

Felix's instincts flared. This was real.

So, naturally, he did something ridiculous.

He waited until the men left, tailed them (badly), snapped a few photos, then spent the next two days digging through old reports, making calls, and doing actual, proper journalism.

And, somehow, it paid off.

Within the week, Felix had uncovered a full-blown financial scandal. Walker had been sitting on documents exposing fraud within the company, millions in misallocated funds, falsified reports, and shady offshore accounts. Felix broke the story before anyone else, and this time, people listened.

Headlines exploded. Investigations were launched. Walker, seeing the writing on the wall had turned whistleblower.

And Felix, for the first time in a long time, was back in the game.

Sure, it had absolutely nothing to do with the Blackwood case. But for once, Felix wasn't the punchline.

And that felt brilliant.

For the first time in a long time, Felix wasn't chasing a lead, second guessing himself, or being laughed at by police officers in the pub. He had done something right. His financial fraud exposé had made headlines, sparked investigations, and for once people were treating him like a journalist instead of a punchline.

So, he decided to take a break.

Felix wasn't great at relaxing, but he gave it a go. He spent a few days not lurking around abandoned estates or breaking into sheds. Instead, he caught up on sleep, went to a café where no one gave him side eyes for eavesdropping, and even managed to sit through an entire film without obsessively checking his notes. He let himself enjoy the rush of success, the satisfaction of getting something right.

But, of course, the question lingered in the back of his mind.

Was it time to go back to the Blackwood case?

It was a mess of dead ends and false leads, a story tangled in layers of mystery that had so far led him nowhere. Maybe it was time to move on. Maybe he should follow up on a fresh case, something winnable, something that wouldn't keep making a fool of him.

And yet... he couldn't shake the feeling that there was something he had missed. Something right in front of him.

He sighed, stirring his coffee absently. Did he really want to dive back into the Blackwood mystery? Or should he chase something else entirely?

Felix had no idea.

But knowing himself, he wouldn't be able to stay away from the Blackwood case for long.

Wrong turn that leads right

Felix's discovery of the police's faked cryptic letter came when he least expected it, and in a way that made him feel both foolish and oddly relieved.

It happened during a routine stop at the local police station. He was just following up on a few loose ends in the Blackwood case that had been simmering in the background, as usual. The place was bustling with the kind of noise that only a station could make, a chaotic blend of ringing phones, ringing voices, and the occasional slam of a file drawer. Felix had an unshakable sense of being the outsider.

He had been chatting with a contact in one of the back offices, trying to pry more information out of them, when something seemingly unrelated caught his attention. He was just about to leave, feeling like he had gotten nowhere once again, when a uniformed officer walked past him holding a stack of papers. One of the pages slipped free, fluttering to the floor.

Felix's instincts kicked in. He had already told himself that he wouldn't be the kind of journalist who pried into things that didn't belong to him. But the paper was right there, and he couldn't help himself. Without a second thought, he picked it up.

It was a printout of the very same cryptic letter, the one that had sent him chasing down rabbit holes for days. The letter that had seemed so mysterious, so carefully worded, as though it were a key to unlocking the Blackwood case.

It wasn't from Eleanor Blackwood.

Felix's heart sank.

He turned the paper over to the back. And there, in the corner, were scribbled initials and a date that looked almost too casual. It didn't take Felix long to piece it together: the letter wasn't a cry for help from Eleanor, it was part of some internal police prank.

He stared at the letter. This was a joke. One that had somehow passed under his radar. The police, in their infinite wisdom, had sent him on a wild goose chase.

It didn't take Felix long to confront the officer about it. When he did, the man just laughed, clearly knowing what was coming. "Oh, that? Yeah, a bit of fun on the side. We figured you'd go nuts over it."

Felix's blood boiled. It wasn't just the fact that they had played him, it was that he had played right into their hands. He'd been so eager to find something real, so desperate to crack the case, that he hadn't stopped to question it. And now, he couldn't unsee it.

He stormed out of the station, trying to ignore the sting of embarrassment. It wasn't the first time he'd been misled. But this time, it had been far too easy. And it stung.

Sitting alone in his flat, Felix let himself think, not about the next lead, not about the next chase, but about everything that had happened so far. He had spent weeks stumbling through dead ends, chasing clues that led nowhere, and making a complete fool of himself more times than he cared to count. But somehow, he had still managed to do something right. That had to mean something.

He had always prided himself on being sharp, on being able to see through lies and deception, yet he had spent most of this case being led in circles. He had been so sure he was on the brink of something big, only to realise that the people around him, sometimes even the ones pretending to help, were either laughing at him or using him for their own amusement. The police's fake cryptic letter had been a wakeup call. He had been so eager to find meaning in it, so convinced it was a crucial clue, that he never stopped to question whether it was real in the first place. But he had to admit, he had done it to himself.

Then there was the note he found in the house. He had convinced himself it was a key piece of the puzzle. But when he had looked, really looked, he had seen the truth staring back at him the entire time. The whole thing had been a trick, a fabrication of his own mind, and yet, he had built entire theories around it. That realisation had hit him harder than he wanted to admit. He was supposed to be the one who uncovered the truth.

Still, it wasn't all failure. The financial fraud case had proven that he wasn't entirely hopeless. When he had stopped looking for mysteries and just focused on the facts, he had done something good. Something that mattered. Maybe that was the real problem, maybe he had been so caught up in trying to make sense of the Blackwood case, in trying to solve the unsolvable, that he had stopped thinking like a journalist.

Felix ran a hand over his face and exhaled slowly. He wasn't sure what that meant for him now. The Blackwood case still tugged at him, still whispered that he had unfinished business. But was it worth it? He wasn't sure.

What he did know was that he needed to start thinking differently. Stop chasing shadows. Stop looking for answers that weren't there. If he was going to continue, he had to do it the right way.

No more chasing unsubstantiated clues. No more letting himself be led around like an idiot.

Next time, he would be the one holding the strings.

Felix had been driving for what felt like hours, his mind back tangled in the mess of the Blackwood case, when he made a wrong turn.

It wasn't even a conscious decision, just a momentary lapse in concentration. His mind had been running through everything, the cryptic letter, the dead end leads, the police joke, and he had somehow made a turn that wasn't on his planned route.

He cursed under his breath as he realised his mistake, pulling over to check the map. The location he thought was crucial to solving the case was a small town barely mentioned in any of the reports he had read. The GPS on his phone flashed a message telling him to turn back, but he didn't bother. He was already far enough off course now.

So, instead of turning back, he decided to keep driving. Maybe he'd discover something unexpected, something the case had been hiding.

A few miles down the road, Felix came across a stretch of woods. The trees stood tall and dense, casting shadows that seemed to stretch endlessly. He wasn't sure what compelled him, but he turned off the main road and drove deeper into the trees. It wasn't the route he was supposed to take, but something about the area felt unusual, in a way that piqued his interest.

The deeper he went, the more the road began to narrow, until it felt like he was driving on nothing more than a dirt path. He nearly turned around several times, but something kept urging him to push forward. Maybe it was the lingering feeling that the Blackwood case was more than just a random disappearance, maybe it was something buried beneath the surface, waiting to be uncovered.

Then, out of nowhere, he saw it.

A small, dilapidated farmhouse, its windows boarded up and the roof sagging from years of neglect. It looked like the kind of place that no one would bother with anymore, but Felix couldn't shake the feeling that it was exactly where he needed to be, and the GPS on his phone confirmed it.

He pulled up slowly, heart racing, wondering why he hadn't visited this place before. There was no real mention of it, or at least not as a place of real significance in any of his files. Yet, everything about the scene felt right.

Felix got out of the car, the eerie quiet of the woods settling in around him. The air smelled faintly of damp earth and decay. He approached the house cautiously, running his hand along the weathered wood of the porch, his instincts tingling with the sense that something important had been hidden here for far too long.

He paused, eyes scanning the surroundings. There, partially obscured by overgrown bushes, was a rusted metal sign that seemed to be half forgotten by time. It read: "Blackwood Farm."

Felix's heart skipped a beat.

It was a twist of fate, he had accidentally arrived at the exact location he needed to be at, even though it was via a slightly different route, he was now at the place that might hold the answers to everything he had been searching for. He had taken a wrong turn, but somehow, it was the right one.

For once, luck had finally decided to work in his favour.

Felix stepped carefully around the farmhouse, the crunch of dead leaves beneath his boots the only sound breaking the silence. He wasn't sure what he was expecting to find, perhaps nothing at all, but the sense of foreboding hung heavily in the air, as though the house itself was waiting for him to uncover its secrets.

The first thing he noticed was how isolated the place felt. Hidden deep in the woods, far off the beaten path, it seemed as though no one had lived here for years. The windows were boarded up, the door partially ajar, as though inviting him inside, or daring him to enter.

Felix's instincts, usually tinged with suspicion, told him to be careful. This wasn't just an old, abandoned farmhouse. It was something else, something more connected to the Blackwood case than he could yet comprehend.

He hesitated for a moment before pushing the door open. The hinges creaked loudly, protesting the movement after years of stillness. Inside, the air was thick with dust, and the stale smell of forgotten memories filled the room. It looked like no one had set foot in the house in ages, yet Felix couldn't shake the feeling that he wasn't alone.

As he moved through the dimly lit interior, something caught his eye. There on the wooden floor by the fireplace was a small chest. Its metal latch was rusted, but it wasn't locked. Felix knelt, brushing aside the debris that had accumulated over the years. His hands trembled slightly as he opened the chest, revealing its contents.

Inside was a stack of old papers, yellowed with age and slightly torn at the edges. Felix carefully flipped through them, his heart racing with every page. They were documents, legal papers, and photographs, fragments of something bigger. A family's history. A series of transactions.

But as Felix scanned the pages, one photograph caught his eye. It was a picture of Eleanor Blackwood, unmistakably young and standing with a man he didn't recognise. They were smiling, posed in front of what looked like the same farmhouse. There was something about him that didn't seem right.

His gut twisted. The man looked eerily familiar. It wasn't until Felix flipped to another page that he recognised him, one of the names he had encountered before, buried deep in the Blackwood case files. The name had been redacted in most of the documents, hidden behind the veil of secrecy, but here, in this forgotten chest, it was clear.

The man in the photograph was George Blackwood.

Felix's mind raced. This was no coincidence. The farmhouse, the documents, the photograph, everything was pointing to a connection that he had completely overlooked before. Eleanor's disappearance. The mysteries that had surrounded her family. And now, a forgotten farmhouse hiding the answers.

But there was still more. As he dug deeper into the chest, his fingers brushed against something cold and hard. He pulled out a small, tarnished key. It was unmarked, plain, and seemed insignificant, yet Felix felt an undeniable pull toward it. What did it unlock? And how was it tied to the secrets of the Blackwood family?

Felix stood up slowly, the discovery settling on his shoulders.

Felix carefully packed the papers, the photograph, and the small, tarnished key into his bag, making sure to handle everything with care. As he stood there, the farmhouse seemed to watch him, its decaying walls almost as though they were reluctant to let him leave with what he had uncovered. But he wasn't about to stay any longer than he had to.

The weight of the documents and the key felt heavy in his bag, both literally and figuratively. Each item felt like a piece of a puzzle that was starting to make sense, and yet, the more pieces he gathered, the more questions seemed to arise. The connection to George Blackwood, the hidden history of the family, and the significance of the key, it was all a mystery he couldn't afford to leave unsolved.

As Felix stepped outside, the crisp air hit him like a wave, the coolness of the evening sharpening his thoughts. He looked back at the farmhouse, its windows staring blankly into the woods, but he didn't linger. There was nothing left for him there, not unless he returned with more answers.

He made his way back to his car, the sound of his footsteps muffled by the thick blanket of fallen leaves. As he slid into the driver's seat, he took a deep breath and glanced over the contents he had found. There was still so much left to uncover, but now, he had the feeling that he was closer than ever to something significant.

He wasn't sure what the key unlocked, but there was a certainty in his gut that it would lead him to the next step.

With the engine running, Felix set off with the past few hours settling into his bones.

He Knows too much

Felix sat across from Detective Harrington in a dimly lit café, his fingers wrapped around a cup of coffee. He had debated whether to meet, but curiosity, and frustration, had won out. If anyone in law enforcement knew the truth about the Blackwood case, it was Harrington. And if Felix had learned anything over the years, it was that people loved to talk, especially when they thought they were the smartest person in the room.

"I've been looking into the farmhouse outside town" Felix said, watching for a reaction. "It was connected to George Blackwood. Found some interesting things there."

Harrington raised an eyebrow, unimpressed. "And?"

"And it looks like the case might not be as closed as everyone thinks" Felix continued. He leaned forward slightly, lowering his voice. "I found documents. A key. A photograph of Eleanor Blackwood with George."

Harrington smirked, shaking his head. "You journalists. Always digging up old bones." He took a slow sip of his drink, letting the silence stretch between them before setting the cup down. "You think you're onto something big, don't you?"

Felix studied him carefully. That smirk. That knowing glint in his eye. He had seen it before, on people who thought they had the upper hand. "You tell me" Felix said. "You seem pretty confident."

Harrington leaned back, tapping his fingers against the table. "Let's just say... some of us already know the truth."

Felix's pulse quickened. "So, you do know what happened."

The detective held his gaze for a long moment before a grin broke across his face. "Nah" he said, laughing. "Just messing with you. But you should see your face."

Felix exhaled sharply, barely restraining the urge to throw his coffee at him. "Are you serious?"

"Completely." Harrington took another sip of his drink, looking entirely too pleased with himself. "I mean, yeah, I know about the Blackwood case. Everyone in the department does. It's the kind of thing rookies hear about when they first join. But do I know what really happened? Nope." He shrugged. "And between you and me, I doubt anyone else does either. Not for sure."

Felix ran a hand through his hair, equal parts frustrated and amused. "So, you've got nothing for me?"

"Not a thing" Harrington said, finishing his drink. "But hey, I appreciate the entertainment."

Felix sighed. He had walked in expecting hints at the truth, maybe even a lead. Instead, he'd found another dead end, and a detective with a terrible sense of humour.

But as he got up to leave, something nagged at him. Harrington was messing with him, sure, but what if there was some truth hidden in that? The police had clearly known something all along. Maybe not the full picture, but enough to keep things buried.

Felix sat in his dimly lit flat, the glow of his laptop screen casting long shadows across the cluttered desk. He knew this was risky, but he was past the point of caring. The police had played him for a fool with that cryptic letter, and he wasn't about to let them get away with it. If they had answers, he was going to find them, one way or another.

He activated his VPN, routing his connection through multiple locations to cover his tracks. Then, he pulled out a set of credentials he had acquired through less than official channels. Years of investigative journalism had introduced him to all sorts of people, some of whom had access to things they really shouldn't have. Felix had never used these credentials before, not for something this serious, but he justified it to himself. He wasn't trying to expose sensitive police operations, just looking for files they had likely buried.

His fingers hovered over the keyboard before he typed in the login details. There was a tense pause as the system processed his request. Then, with a soft chime, the screen shifted. He was in.

Felix exhaled slowly, his heart thumping in his chest. He navigated carefully, searching for anything related to George Blackwood or Eleanor's disappearance. Redacted reports, closed case files, internal memos, there had to be something.

Then he found it. A folder labelled Blackwood Investigation – Restricted Access.

His pulse quickened as he clicked. The documents loaded, revealing police reports, interview transcripts, and surveillance logs. One entry caught his eye, a report dated years after Eleanor's disappearance. It mentioned a sighting of George Blackwood, alive and well, well after the world had assumed he was either missing or dead.

Felix leaned back, his mind racing. The police had known. They had found George. And they had covered it up.

Felix didn't waste time. He grabbed his phone and scrolled through his contacts until he found the name he was looking for, Sergeant Lisa Carter. She was one of the few officers he trusted or at least trusted more than the rest. She had given him useful information in the past, always careful never to say too much, but Felix had a feeling she knew more about this than she had ever let on.

He pressed call.

It rang twice before she picked up. "Felix? You know I hate it when you call me this late."

"I'll make it worth your while" he said, glancing at his laptop screen. "I need to ask about George Blackwood."

There was silence on the other end. Then, a sigh. "What about him?"

"You tell me" Felix said. "Why isn't it common knowledge that he was found alive and well?"

Another pause, longer this time. "Where did you hear that?"

"I have my sources" Felix replied vaguely. "But you and I both know I wouldn't be asking if I didn't already have proof. So, Lisa, why was it covered up?"

"I never said it was covered up."

"You didn't have to."

There was a muffled sound on her end, maybe papers shuffling, maybe someone nearby. When she spoke again, her voice was lower, more cautious. "Felix, listen to me. I don't know how you got that information, but if I were you, I'd stop digging."

He sat up straighter. "That sounds like a warning."

"It's advice" she corrected. "The Blackwood case is old news, and if George was found, that means it wasn't relevant anymore. There's nothing to gain from dragging it up again."

Felix clenched his jaw. "Then why wasn't it made public? Why was it kept quiet?"

A beat of silence. Then: "Because sometimes, Felix, the truth doesn't need an audience."

Felix frowned. "That's not good enough."

Lisa sighed again. "I can't help you with this. And if you know what's good for you, you'll leave it alone."

The line went dead.

Felix stared at his phone, gripping it tightly. That hadn't been a denial. She hadn't said he was wrong. If anything, she had just confirmed that something was being hidden.

Felix had barely put his phone down when it buzzed again. Lisa. He hesitated before answering, letting her voice come through first.

"Felix, I'm sorry I was so abrupt" she said, sounding tired. "It's late, and this whole thing... it's complicated."

"Complicated tends to be my speciality" Felix said, though his voice lacked its usual sarcasm.

Lisa sighed. "Look, it wasn't covered up. There was just no need to make an announcement. By the time George was found, the case had already gone cold. No more leads, nothing more to investigate. And at that stage, the family had already suffered enough. Dragging it all back into the public eye wouldn't have done anyone any good."

Felix leaned back in his chair, rubbing a hand over his face. He could understand that, but it still didn't sit right with him. "So that's it? Just let it go?"

"That's what we did" Lisa said gently. "And that's what I'm suggesting you do too."

Felix was quiet for a moment. He knew she meant well, that she was giving him the kind of advice a friend would. But something still felt unfinished. He had spent too long chasing leads, only to find out some of them had never been relevant in the first place.

"You don't have to prove anything, Felix" Lisa added after a moment. "Not every mystery needs to be solved."

Felix let out a small, humourless laugh. "Try telling that to my brain."

Lisa chuckled softly. "Yeah, I figured as much. Just... don't let this one swallow you whole, okay?"

Felix didn't promise anything, but he thanked her before hanging up. He stared at his screen, the police report still open in front of him. He had the truth, or at least one version of it.

Eleanor Blackwood's disappearance had shattered the Blackwood family, thrusting them into the kind of relentless scrutiny that only a high-profile tragedy could bring. The Blackwoods had always been a well-known name, prominent, wealthy, the kind of family that appeared in newspapers for charity galas and business ventures. But after Eleanor vanished, their reputation became something else entirely.

Speculation ran wild. Some believed she had been kidnapped, others whispered about family secrets, and a few even suggested she had run away from something, or someone. Every theory was dissected in the press, every move the family made scrutinised. It was unbearable, especially for Eleanor's parents.

Her mother, Margaret Blackwood, had been a respected woman, known for her charity work and unwavering composure. But after Eleanor disappeared, the once, poised matriarch crumbled under the pressure. The stress of the investigation, the media hounding them at every turn, and the whispered allegations, some even hinting at the family's own involvement, took its toll. She withdrew from public life, refusing interviews, ignoring the phone calls from reporters who wanted their next headline.

Friends said she became a shadow of herself, plagued by grief and guilt. She was convinced that she had missed something, that she should have done more, that she should have known. Some say she died of a broken heart, though the official cause was never listed that way. The strain of losing her daughter had simply been too much.

Not long after, her husband, Richard Blackwood followed. A heart attack they said, but those who knew him believed it was more than that. He had spent so much time fighting, trying to push authorities to keep the investigation open, to not let his daughter be forgotten. The stress had been relentless. Losing Eleanor had broken Margaret and losing both had broken him.

By the time the dust settled, the once powerful Blackwood family was reduced to a tragic story, a cautionary tale of how quickly a name could go from admired to pitied. And through it all, the mystery of Eleanor's disappearance remained, unanswered, unresolved, and still whispering through the cracks of the grand estate they had left behind.

Abandoned

After Richard and Margaret Blackwood passed away, control of the Blackwood estate and the family farm fell to Richard's younger brother, George Blackwood. Technically, most of it belonged to Eleanor, she was the rightful heir, but with her still missing, everything remained in legal limbo.

Unlike his brother, George had never been one for the spotlight. He had always been the quieter one, the less ambitious sibling who preferred a simple life away from public attention. And while he never gave up hope that Eleanor might return one day, he also knew that keeping the estate running meant keeping himself tied to a painful past. The constant intrusion from the press, the never, ending police inquiries, and the morbid curiosity of the public became too much to bear.

He walked away.

He didn't sell the land, nor did he make any grand declarations. He simply left, letting the house and the farm fade into neglect. Time and nature took over, creeping through the cracks and swallowing what was once a proud family home. The grand Blackwood estate became little more than a forgotten relic, a decaying monument to a family that had crumbled under tragedy.

George, however, lived on, peacefully and comfortably, far from the name that once followed him wherever he went. He didn't seek the public eye, and he certainly didn't invite questions. As far as he was concerned, the past was a door he had chosen to close. The world had moved on and so had he.

But some things don't stay buried forever. And whether he liked it or not, the Blackwood name still had unfinished business.

Felix wasn't one to let sleeping dogs lie, not when they might have answers. George Blackwood had vanished from public life, but that didn't mean he was impossible to find. People like George always left a trail, however faint.

Felix started with the obvious. He combed through old property records, looking for any signs that George had officially transferred ownership of anything. Nothing. The estate and farm were registered to a trust, just as they had been for years. No sales, no movement.

He moved on to financial records, at least the ones he could get his hands on. Felix had his ways, a few calls, a few discreet searches, and he got what he needed: George Blackwood wasn't entirely off the grid. There were routine transactions, nothing too extravagant, but consistent, linked to an address outside of town.

A cottage, owned by George, tucked away near the coast.

Felix smirked. The man might have wanted to disappear, but he still had to live somewhere and buy groceries.

With an address in hand, Felix debated his next move. He could try calling, but he doubted George would pick up for an unknown number. A letter might work, but it could also be ignored. No, there was only one real option.

He had to go there himself.

Felix packed a small bag, grabbing the essentials, his notebook, a couple of pens, and a bottle of water. He didn't expect to get any answers quickly, but something about the quiet distance of the location intrigued him. He needed to see it for himself, to find out just how far George Blackwood had really gone to escape his past.

The journey took a couple of hours, winding through small villages and along narrow country roads, the landscape stretching out around him in an unbroken expanse of rolling hills and quiet fields. Felix's mind wandered as he drove, revisiting everything he had uncovered so far, but his thoughts always circled back to George. Why had he chosen this remote place? What had driven him to retreat so completely from the world? And more importantly, what was George hiding?

By the time Felix reached the small cottage, the sun was starting to dip, casting shadows over the unassuming building. It wasn't much, although very pretty, but just really a modest stone structure surrounded by a wild garden. The windows were dark, the door slightly ajar as if it had been left that way deliberately, but there was no sign of life.

Felix pulled over, parking his car a little way down the lane to avoid drawing attention. He wanted to approach cautiously, unsure whether George was home or if the place had been abandoned entirely. The last thing he wanted was to alert George before he had the chance to gather information.

He stood for a moment, taking in the sight of the cottage before he moved closer, his footsteps as silent as possible on the gravel path. The door creaked as he pushed it open further, now just enough to peek inside. The place seemed simple, almost barren in some ways and nothing like the Blackwood estate he had seen earlier. No signs of wealth or grandeur, just a life lived in seclusion.

Felix lingered by the door, trying to decide whether to step inside or wait for a sign.

Felix hesitated for a split second before calling out, his voice carrying across the quiet space. "Hello? George Blackwood?"

There was a moment of silence, then the sound of footsteps approaching the door. Felix stood still, his heart picking up its pace. He wasn't sure how this would go, whether George would be welcoming or defensive, but he needed to make the first move.

George Blackwood came into view, his expression was guarded, his eyes narrowing slightly as he assessed Felix, as though trying to place him.

"Hello, how can I help?" George's voice was calm, but there was an edge to it, like he wasn't sure whether to be concerned or curious.

Felix took a step forward, offering a polite smile that didn't quite reach his eyes. "Mr. Blackwood, I hope I'm not disturbing you. I'm Felix Harrow, an investigative journalist. I've been looking into the Blackwood case, and I understand you've been living here for some time."

George's gaze shifted, his lips tightening slightly. "I didn't know the Blackwood case was still of interest" he said, his tone becoming more guarded. "I thought that chapter was closed."

"It's never that simple, is it?" Felix replied, trying to keep his voice steady. "There are still so many unanswered questions about what happened to your niece, Eleanor. And your sudden disappearance from the public eye raises some... concerns."

George's eyes darkened at the mention of Eleanor's name. He took a slow breath, and for a moment, Felix could see the years of pain and frustration flicker in his expression.

"I've had my reasons for staying out of the spotlight"
George said finally, his voice lower now. "The family's been
through enough, don't you think?"

Felix didn't back down. "I agree. But there's still a story
here, George. A lot of things don't add up, and I think you
might know more than you're letting on."

There was a pause before George stepped aside, opening
the door fully. "If you're so determined to find the truth,
you'd better come inside."

Felix took a deep breath, stepping over the threshold.
Whatever he was about to uncover, he had to be ready for
it.

Inside the cottage, Felix sat across from George in a
modest living room. The small room was sparsely
furnished, nothing extravagant, just a few chairs, a coffee
table, and shelves lined with old books and photographs,
a far cry from the life the family enjoyed at the Blackwood
estate.

The conversation began slowly, but as Felix asked
questions, George seemed to open up, as if the floodgates
had finally been unlocked.

"It was a nightmare" George said, rubbing his hands over
his face, as though trying to push away the memories. "I
never imagined the kind of torment we'd go through. The
press, the speculation, it was unbearable. Eleanor was our
family, our blood, and to have her disappear without a

trace, to have our name dragged through the mud... I wouldn't wish it on anyone."

Felix nodded, taking it all in. He had heard of the Blackwoods' suffering from the media but hearing it from someone who had lived through it was different. "You tried everything, though. Private investigators, expensive ones, at great cost, and still nothing?"

George's lips twisted into a bitter smile. "We hired the best Felix. People with reputations for cracking cases like this. They turned up nothing. We had all the police resources, too. But no leads. No breakthroughs. Just dead ends. It was like she had vanished into thin air."

Felix glanced down at the floor, watching the reflection of the dim light as it played across the old wooden boards. "And then the accusations?" he asked quietly.

"Don't get me started" George replied, his voice tight. "People can be cruel when they don't understand. They've always been quick to assume the worst. The whispers about the family, about Richard, about Margaret... even about me. People saying things I wouldn't repeat. It was a nightmare. A grieving family turned into the subject of gossip."

There was a long silence, both sitting in the heaviness of the conversation. George eventually spoke again, his voice softer. "I would've given anything for things to turn out differently. For Eleanor to come home safe. To have that part of our lives back."

Felix could hear the deep regret in his tone, and he realised, for all his years of investigation, he had never quite understood what it was like to lose someone so completely. The pain wasn't just in the unknown, it was in the constant reminders that life moved on, and you were left standing still, trapped in a moment of tragedy.

George leaned back in his chair, his eyes distant, as if reliving every painful memory. "But things are as they are now. The police had their time, the investigators had theirs, and still... nothing. The case went cold, and the rest of us had to keep going. We can't change that. But if you..." He paused, his gaze finally meeting Felix's. "If you can uncover what happened, if you can find the answers that no one else could, I'd welcome it. I'd be grateful. Because the truth, whatever it may be, is better than living in the dark forever."

Felix studied George carefully. There was no hostility, no defensiveness, just a quiet acceptance of the past and a deep desire for closure. It was a rare thing to find in someone who had suffered so much.

"I'll do what I can" Felix said after a long pause. "But I can't promise anything. What I've uncovered so far doesn't make sense. And there are too many questions still lingering. But I'll keep looking. You deserve the truth."

George nodded slowly, his expression grateful but weary. "I never wanted to leave the past behind, Felix. But sometimes... it's all you can do."

Felix understood. It wasn't about the past anymore, or the search for the truth alone. It was about finding peace. For George, and for the Blackwood family, if only they could finally lay this situation to rest.

A great day out

George's invitation came unexpectedly, but it was clear there was more to this gesture than just sharing a meal. Felix couldn't help but feel a strange sense of gratitude, a sort of unspoken bond forming between them.

"Join me for lunch" George said, standing up from his chair and brushing his hands together as if dismissing the seriousness of their earlier conversation. "I'm meeting with a friend, and anyone who is looking for the truth of what happened to Eleanor is a friend of mine."

Felix nodded, feeling both humbled and curious. "I'd appreciate that."

George led the way to a small kitchen at the back of the cottage, its windows looking out over a patch of wild garden that seemed untouched by time. The rustic feel of the room was inviting, and despite its simplicity, there was an undeniable warmth to it.

As they worked together to prepare a simple meal, some local bread, cheese, and cold cuts, Felix couldn't help but wonder about the "friend" George was meeting. He knew it wasn't just a casual lunch. George had invited them for a reason, and it wasn't lost on him that the timing of the invitation felt purposeful.

"I've been thinking about what you said" George continued as he placed the plates on the table. "About uncovering the truth. It's not just for me Felix. It's for everyone who's been affected by Eleanor's disappearance, her friends, the staff who worked at the estate, even the people who lived in the town. They all want closure, even if they don't say it."

Felix gave a small, thoughtful nod, realising how much more this case had become about than just the Blackwood family. The ripples of Eleanor's disappearance had touched so many lives in ways he hadn't even considered.

"Let's hope you're right" Felix said, taking a seat at the small kitchen table. "Maybe the truth will be enough for everyone to move on."

George's eyes met his, the quiet sadness in them telling a story of years spent searching for something that may never have a simple answer. "I hope so, too."

The doorbell rang, breaking the moment of silence. George looked up, his eyes glinting with an unreadable expression. "Ah, there's my friend now."

Felix's curiosity spiked. Who was this person, and what did they know about Eleanor's disappearance? Would they have the key to unlocking the mystery, or was George about to share something Felix wasn't ready to hear?

The atmosphere shifted as the door opened and a new presence entered the room, easy going, relaxed, and carrying with them an air of familiarity. Felix took a quiet moment to observe as George greeted the newcomer with a friendly kiss, hug, and a smile. There was no tension, no trace of the conversation that had preceded this moment. It was as though the previous conversation had never happened, replaced instead by the light-hearted exchange between old friends.

"Felix, this is Claire" George said, motioning to the woman now taking a seat at the table. "We've known each other for years, and she's been a constant in my life, especially after everything that happened with Eleanor."

Felix extended his hand, offering a polite smile. "Nice to meet you, Claire."

"Likewise" she replied with a warm grin. Her voice was friendly, and her easy manner immediately put Felix at ease. She had the kind of personality that filled the room without dominating it, and it was clear that she and George were comfortable with one another.

They all sat down together, and the meal began. There was no talk of police investigations, no speculation about Eleanor or the Blackwood family history. Instead, the conversation flowed naturally, light-hearted, and casual. They spoke of recent events, making jokes about the weather, about town gossip, and about the oddities of the local community. Claire shared stories of her recent travels, while George recounted some comical incidents at a local pub. Felix listened intently, occasionally chiming in with his own anecdotes, but always aware that he was a guest at the table.

The meal itself was simple but satisfying, a hearty spread of bread, cheese, meats, and fresh vegetables. The warmth of the food, coupled with the relaxed pace of the meal, created an inviting atmosphere, one that made Felix feel as though he was being welcomed into something larger than just a shared lunch. It wasn't just about the meal, it was about the ease of good company.

As they ate, the conversation turned to future. Claire spoke excitedly about a project she was working on, while George, more reserved, seemed content to listen and offer support. Felix couldn't help but notice how much they enjoyed one another's company, the way they shared memories and dreams for what lay ahead. The laughter in the room was genuine, the kind of laughter that only old friends could share.

Felix felt himself relaxing more with each passing minute, his thoughts momentarily drifting from the case. This was what life could be like, he thought, free of unanswered questions, the constant pursuit of elusive truths. For this moment, there was no Blackwood mystery, no cryptic letters, no hidden clues. There was just a meal, shared with people who truly valued each other's presence.

It was only when the meal ended, and the conversation shifted again back into more comfortable territory that Felix realised how much he'd needed this. A brief escape, even if it was only for a few hours had allowed him to reset. But it also left him wondering if this same sense of peace would be possible if he were to ever find the answers he was seeking about the Blackwood family?

For now, he was content to simply enjoy the company.

As the evening drew on, the warmth from the meal lingered, and the casual conversations flowed effortlessly into the evening. Claire was the first to notice the time glancing at the clock on the wall before she excused herself with a gentle smile.

"I should get going" she said, standing up from the table. "I've got an early start tomorrow, and I don't want to keep you both up." She looked over at Felix with a friendly nod. "It was really nice meeting you Felix."

"Likewise" Felix replied, offering a polite smile. "Take care."

As Claire gathered her things, Felix and George exchanged a few casual words. Once Claire had left, George turned to Felix, his face betraying a hint of weariness mixed with warmth.

"I'm glad you could join us" George said, his voice lowering slightly. "It's been a while since I've had someone new around to just... talk with. And you've been a good listener."

Felix nodded, appreciating the sentiment. He wasn't used to being on the receiving end of this sort of compliment, especially not from someone with as much history as George.

"You're welcome. It's been a pleasant change of pace" Felix replied, smiling faintly.

George moved toward the door. "Well, if you're not in a rush to leave, you're more than welcome to stay the night. There's a spare room here. You can head out in the morning, whenever you're ready."

Felix paused, considering the offer. The night had turned colder, and he realised how much more comfortable it would be to rest here rather than drive back through the dark, empty countryside. Plus, it would give him more time to think, time away from the case, time to process everything that had happened so far.

"That's generous of you, George" Felix said, nodding thoughtfully. "I'd appreciate that."

"Good" George said with a smile, looking relieved. "Let me show you to your room. There's some tea if you want, and we can chat more in the morning if you feel like it."

Felix followed George upstairs. The house felt different now, warmer, more inviting than it had when he first arrived. It was clear George had chosen to live quietly away from the chaos of the past. It made Felix wonder if there was peace to be found here, in this forgotten corner of the world. But he didn't linger too long on that thought, knowing that tomorrow would bring him one step closer to unravelling the mystery of Eleanor Blackwood's disappearance.

As George showed him the room, Felix couldn't help but feel a strange sense of gratitude. He'd walked into this house as a stranger, but the hospitality and openness had made him feel welcome. And in a way, that felt like a small victory.

"Rest well" George said with a smile, before leaving Felix to settle in. "We'll see what the morning brings."

Felix nodded, the quiet of the house settling around him as he closed the door and began to prepare for another day of searching for answers.

As Felix lay in the bed, the darkness of the room enveloping him, his mind began to wander. The events of the day, of the Blackwood estate, of George's quiet life away from the chaos, mingled with the questions that still loomed large in his thoughts. The mystery of Eleanor's disappearance had a strangle hold on him, one that refused to loosen, even in his dreams.

Gradually, he drifted into a deep, heavy sleep.

In his dream, he found himself on a sunlit beach, the sound of waves lapping gently at the shore. The sun was warm on his face, and the air smelled faintly of saltwater. He turned to see George standing beside him, a relaxed smile on his face, years of grief momentarily lifted. It was as if the world had paused, and Felix could breathe without the suffocating pressure of the case hanging over him.

"This is nice" Felix said, feeling a sense of peace he hadn't felt in months.

George nodded, his hands in his pockets. "Sometimes it's good to take a break from the things we can't control. Maybe that's why you're here."

Felix glanced around, realising that the beach stretched endlessly before them with no sign of anything that would disrupt the calm. It was an idyllic scene, too perfect, too unreal. But still, something in his gut told him it wasn't simply a holiday. This wasn't just a break. There was something they were supposed to find.

As the dream shifted, the setting changed. The beach was gone, replaced by an old overgrown mansion, the Blackwood estate, just as Felix had seen it before, but with an air of mystery that hung around it like a fog. It loomed tall and ominous in the distance, its windows dark, its doors shut tight. Yet, in the dream, it didn't feel threatening.

Felix turned to George, who was already walking towards the estate with a determined step. He felt an impulse to follow, the nagging sense that this was the key, the reason for the disappearance, the answer that had been eluding him.

As they approached the house, the front door creaked open on its own. Inside, the mansion was quiet, but it was filled with an odd sense of familiarity. They stepped across the threshold, and Felix felt a shiver run down his spine. The house wasn't abandoned, it was alive with memories.

They moved through the hallways exploring the rooms one by one. The air was thick with the remnants of the past. It was only when they reached the old study, Eleanor's father's study, that they found what they were looking for.

In the centre of the room was a small, faded desk, its wood cracked with age. On the desk was a single letter, its contents smudged but still legible. Felix reached for it, his hand trembling as he unfolded the paper. The words on the page were cryptic, but there was one thing that stood out, a name, written in the corner: "George."

Before Felix could make sense of the meaning, a voice echoed through the house, soft but clear. "You were looking for answers Felix, but the truth was here all along."

Felix turned to find George standing by the window, his expression unreadable. "The truth isn't what you think it is. Eleanor didn't disappear, she left, because she had to."

Felix woke with a start, the remnants of the dream still clinging to his mind like a fog. The room around him was dark, quiet, and still. The dream had felt so real, yet he knew it had been nothing more than his mind playing tricks on him.

Still, something about the final words echoed in his thoughts: "*The truth was here all along.*" And that cryptic letter with George's name written on it, what did it mean? What had Eleanor known, and why had she left?

Felix lay back in bed, his mind racing. He knew it wasn't just a dream, it was a clue, hidden in the subconscious layers of his mind. Whatever had happened to Eleanor, it wasn't as straightforward as he had believed. Maybe, just maybe, the answers he sought had been staring him in the face all along.

More of the same

Felix slowly woke, the remnants of his previous dream still lingering in his mind, though fading as he became more aware of his surroundings. He could hear the soft clink of pots and pans from downstairs, the comforting aroma of cooking food drifting up through the floorboards. His stomach rumbled, a quiet reminder that the world outside his thoughts was moving on, indifferent to his internal turmoil.

He took a moment to stretch, his body still heavy with sleep, but there was something grounding about the noise from below. It was an ordinary sound, something that signified comfort and familiarity, breakfast being made, the start of another day.

Felix rubbed his eyes and sat up, blinking away the remnants of his dream. He wasn't sure what it meant, or why the dream had been so vivid, but the cryptic letter with George's name stuck with him, the lingering question gnawing at him. He could feel the pull to figure it out, to understand the connection, but for now, he'd need to set those thoughts aside. Breakfast was waiting, and perhaps a fresh start would give him some clarity.

He threw on his clothes and made his way downstairs, where the smell of fried eggs, toast, and bacon greeted him like an old friend. George was standing at the stove, humming softly to himself, looking relaxed and at ease, as though the previous evening's heaviness had lifted entirely.

"Morning Felix" George called over his shoulder as Felix entered the kitchen. "You're just in time. I hope you're hungry."

Felix smiled, the simplicity of the moment soothing his frayed nerves. "It smells great" he said, settling at the kitchen table. "I didn't realise you were such a master chef."

George chuckled. "Hardly. But I can handle a decent breakfast. We'll see if you're still saying that after I serve you."

Felix laughed softly, feeling a brief flicker of normalcy. As George set a plate down in front of him, filled with a hearty breakfast, Felix couldn't help but let the thoughts of his investigation slip away. The calm of the morning, the warmth of the meal, and the casual conversation made it easy to forget the gnawing question that had been on his mind, the one about Eleanor, the letter, and the mystery that seemed to grow with every passing day.

But as he ate, Felix couldn't entirely push the thoughts aside. His dream, the cryptic letter, and the strange sense that he was on the edge of something bigger continued to pulse in the back of his mind. He knew that before long, he would have to dive back into the case. But for now, the simple joy of breakfast and good company was enough to hold him over.

"Thanks for this, George" Felix said, taking another bite. "It's just what I needed."

George smiled, his eyes reflecting a quiet understanding. "Anytime, Felix. Anytime."

"If you have nothing planned today, why don't you join me for a trip into town? I have a few errands to run, and you can do some sightseeing, maybe we can catch a movie too!"

Felix looked up from his plate, surprised but pleasantly so by George's offer. He hadn't expected such a casual invitation, but the idea of a day away from the looming Blackwood mystery and a chance to clear his head was tempting.

"That sounds like a great idea" Felix replied, pushing his empty plate aside. "I don't have anything pressing at the moment, and I could definitely use a change of scenery. A movie sounds good too. What's showing?"

George grinned as he started cleaning up, his movements relaxed and confident, as though the offer had been a natural part of his day. "There's a little independent cinema in town. They've got some classic films on rotation, nothing big or flashy, but it's a good escape. As for the errands, nothing too exciting. Just some accounts to settle and a few small things I need from the shop."

Felix nodded, intrigued by the simplicity of the plan. A day spent in town with no immediate worries seemed like a welcome break from his usual routine of investigating. It was hard to remember the last time he'd had a chance to be a normal person, just enjoying the moment without being consumed by a case.

"I'd be happy to join you" Felix said. "It'll be nice to just take a step back for a while."

After a few more minutes of cleaning up, George gave a satisfied nod. "Great, then let's head out in a bit. I'll grab my coat, and we can be on our way."

Felix followed George to the front door, the cool morning air greeting them as they stepped outside. It was a refreshing change from the intensity of the past few days, and the thought of exploring a quiet town without any sense of urgency was almost too good to pass up.

As they drove toward the town, Felix allowed himself to let go of his concerns, even if just for a few hours. He couldn't shake the feeling that the answers to the Blackwood case were still waiting for him, but for the time being, he would let the town, and the movie fill his mind.

As they drove through the winding roads towards town, the countryside stretching out on either side, George's words came unexpectedly, yet naturally. He glanced over at Felix, his hands on the wheel, a thoughtful expression on his face.

"You know, Felix" George said casually "I've come to realise that living in the now is one of the best things you can do. The past can eat you up if you let it, drag you into regret. And the future? Well, it pulls you in with worry, constantly wondering what might happen next."

Felix listened intently, a little surprised at the depth of George's reflection, given the laid-back nature of their morning. It was clear that George had found peace in something Felix was still grappling with, how to deal with his past mistakes, and how to face the unknown that lay ahead in the Blackwood case.

George continued, his gaze still focused on the road ahead. "It took me a long time to realise that. I spent years holding onto the past, thinking about Eleanor, about what could have been. But in the end, you can't change it can you? You can't go back and fix things. And the future… well, it's always there, waiting to surprise you, but you can't live in it. You must take each day as it comes."

Felix nodded, letting George's words settle in his mind. It was a philosophy that made sense, and one that Felix often struggled with. He was always looking ahead, hunting for the next clue, the next lead, and often found himself unable to relax, unable to let go of the past.

"I suppose that's true" Felix said slowly. "I get so caught up in chasing answers, chasing justice, that I forget to just... be. The case, the investigation, it all starts to take over. But maybe I need to take a step back and think about today. What's right in front of me, not what's behind me or ahead."

George smiled, his eyes crinkling at the edges. "Exactly. Sometimes, the best way to move forward is to simply live in the present. Enjoy the moment. And right now, the moment is here. A trip to town, a movie, a meal. Tomorrow will come, but for today, just be in it."

Felix couldn't help but feel a small sense of relief, as though George had given him permission to breathe. Maybe it wasn't all about finding the answer to the Blackwood mystery right away. Maybe the key to solving it, to understanding it, lay in letting go for a while. To enjoy the small, everyday things that had been slipping through his fingers as he chased something intangible.

"Thanks George" Felix said quietly. "I think I needed to hear that."

George chuckled lightly, his fingers tapping on the steering wheel to a tune only he could hear. "We all do sometimes."

Felix smiled, feeling the tension in his shoulders ease just a little. It wasn't much, but for the first time in days, it felt like he could allow himself to just be. To take things one step at a time, and maybe, in doing so, find the answers he'd been chasing.

Felix wandered through the small town, taking in the sights of the quaint shops that lined the streets. Each window seemed to tell its own story, handmade crafts, old books with frayed spines, an assortment of clothing. The air was crisp and fresh, the kind of weather that made every step feel like a moment to savour. He browsed at a leisurely pace, admiring the local artwork in one gallery, sifting through old records in a music shop, and even picking up a small trinket to remember the day by.

Meanwhile, George had been running errands, disappearing into various shops, but Felix didn't mind the time to himself. It was a rare opportunity to simply exist, to soak in the rhythm of small-town life. His mind, which had been racing with the Blackwood case for so long, finally felt quiet. The day was about simplicity, no mysteries to solve, no clues to chase, just time spent taking in the world.

After a couple of hours, they regrouped at a small, independent cinema in the heart of town. The flickering images on the screen were a welcome escape, the old film a stark contrast to what Felix had been carrying in his daily life. He found himself laughing and relaxed, not thinking about the past or the future, but just enjoying the moment. The film ended, and they left the theatre, feeling content.

"I'm glad we did this" Felix said, stretching as they walked towards a nearby restaurant. "I honestly didn't realise how much I needed the break."

George smiled, a warmth in his voice. "Sometimes, the best way to get answers is to step away from the problem for a while. Trust me, you'll see things clearer when you're not so focused on them."

The two entered the cosy restaurant, a homely place with checkered floors and the aroma of fresh cooking in the air. They sat at a corner table by the window, a perfect spot to watch the world outside, still buzzing with the quiet energy of the afternoon. The waiter brought them menus, but George had already made up his mind.

"Let's go with the special" George said. "And don't worry about the bill, Felix. It's on me today."

Felix raised an eyebrow, surprised. "You sure? I can "

"Nope" George interrupted, waving a hand. "Consider it my treat. You've been a good sport today, and besides, you're going to need all your energy for the next part of the day."

Felix laughed, a little taken aback by George's generosity. "Well, I'm not going to argue with that."

They ate, chatting about everything and nothing, light conversation about local happenings, stories from the past, and a few jokes that had Felix chuckling. It felt so normal, so far removed from the investigation that had been dominating his thoughts. It was a reminder that life wasn't just about searching for answers, it was also about these moments of connection, of stepping away from the chase and living in the present.

As the meal wound down, Felix felt something he hadn't in a long while: a sense of peace. The Blackwood case was still there, looming in the background, but for a few hours, it had taken a backseat. He didn't know when he'd return to the investigation, or what the next step would be, but for now, he could rest.

As they left the restaurant, George clapped him on the back with a grin. "Now, let's see what else the day holds. But remember, no stress. We'll get to whatever's next when the time comes."

Felix smiled, feeling a little lighter than when the day began. He wasn't sure how much more of the mystery he could unravel, but for now, he was content. The Blackwood case, much like the rest of life, would wait until he was ready to face it again.

Back to reality

As they made their way back to George's house, the afternoon sun cast a warm golden glow over the landscape. The peaceful town, now quiet in the late afternoon, seemed a world away from the chaos Felix had been mired in for the past few weeks. It was a refreshing change, and the lightness of the day was something he wouldn't easily forget.

They arrived at the house, and Felix could feel the day's calm settling over him. It had been a perfect escape, even if only for a brief time. The hum of the house felt more comforting now, the silence somehow more reassuring than it had been before.

"Thanks again George" Felix said, turning to his friend as he unbuckled his seatbelt. "Today really helped, more than you know. I needed the break."

George smiled warmly, his eyes crinkling at the edges. "You're welcome, Felix. Sometimes, you've got to step back to move forward. And if there's anything you need, anything at all, don't hesitate to reach out."

Felix nodded, appreciating the sentiment. It wasn't often that he had someone who understood how vital those moments of peace were, especially when you were wrapped up in a case that refused to let go.

"I'll keep that in mind" Felix replied. "It's been a pleasure, really. I wasn't sure what to expect when I came here, but I'm glad I did."

The two of them stood there for a moment, the quiet of the house wrapping around them. George clasped his hands behind his back, a thoughtful expression on his face.

"Take care, Felix" George said, a hint of finality in his voice. "You've got a lot ahead of you, but don't let it wear you down."

Felix offered a small smile, grateful for the kindness. "I'll keep that in mind as well. Thanks again."

As he gathered his things and prepared for the long journey back, Felix couldn't help but reflect on the day. It had been a brief reprieve, but in many ways, it had given him something he'd been missing - perspective. George had reminded him that there was more to life than the endless pursuit of answers. Maybe he didn't need to solve everything in a day, and maybe taking a step back from the Blackwood case would be the key to seeing things clearly again.

As Felix continued his journey back home, the peacefulness of the day slowly began to dissipate, replaced by the familiar hum of his thoughts. At first, it was subtle, a passing idea, a flicker of doubt, but soon enough, it was like a switch had been flipped. His mind, so content just moments ago, started to churn again, one thought tumbling after another.

His fingers drummed lightly on the steering wheel, and his gaze flicked between the road and the view outside. The Blackwood case, which had been temporarily buried, began to resurface. The questions, the clues, the pieces of the puzzle he had yet to fit together, they were all back, swirling in his mind.

What had happened to Eleanor? Why had George been so willing to let go of the past, to leave everything behind so easily? And the strange turn of events, the cryptic letters, the quiet murmurs of things left unsaid, none of it made sense. It was all connected somehow, but the pieces weren't falling into place.

Felix sighed, gripping the wheel a little tighter. He couldn't help it. It was in his nature to keep digging, to keep pursuing, even when it seemed like he was getting nowhere. The Blackwood family, George and Eleanor's disappearance, there was a story there. But the more he thought about it, the more he realised that the answers might not be what he expected. In fact, they might be something he'd missed all along.

George had talked about living in the present, letting go of the past, and Felix couldn't deny the wisdom in it. But at the same time, he couldn't just abandon the case. There was something still pulling at him, something in his gut telling him that there was more to uncover.

His mind bounced between possibilities, each one feeding into the next. Maybe George had been hiding something. Or maybe it was something in Eleanor's past that no one had thought to question. Perhaps there was more to her disappearance than just a tragedy, a secret buried deep within the family, one that no one had dared speak of.

The road ahead stretched out in front of him, but Felix didn't notice. His mind was elsewhere, back at the farmhouse, back with George, back with the puzzle pieces that were still scattered and waiting to be put together. It was frustrating, but he couldn't let it go.

The more he tried to push the thoughts aside, the louder they became. Felix had learned a long time ago that the key to solving any case, any mystery, was persistence. And right now, that meant not letting go of the questions that still lingered in the air, unanswered.

Before he knew it, he had driven miles past his intended turn-off, the road ahead now unfamiliar, as his mind raced further into the labyrinth of his thoughts. Felix had never been one to ignore a hunch, and right now, his instincts were telling him there was something more, something he had missed. And no matter how much he tried to ignore it, he knew he wouldn't rest until he found the answers.

Felix shook his head, trying to clear his thoughts as he turned the car around, the unfamiliar road stretching behind him. His focus shifted now, he had to make sure he was heading in the right direction, get back to his own life, and let the case rest for the night. But despite the reassuring hum of the engine, his mind was anything but settled.

George's attitude had stuck with him. The way George had seemed so detached about the past, almost as if it didn't matter. It was as though Eleanor's disappearance, the family's tragedy, was something that had been so thoroughly buried that even the faintest mention of it was uncomfortable for him. Felix had brushed it off earlier, thinking George was simply a man who had learned to live with the pain and the unanswered questions.

But now, as Felix steered the car back onto the familiar road, a creeping suspicion gnawed at him. Was George really so at peace with the situation? Was he so willing to move on because he had let go, or because he had something to hide? The more Felix thought about it, the more George's calm, nonchalant attitude seemed to raise questions.

Had George just grown tired of the constant media frenzy? The unrelenting pressure from the police? Or was there something more to his indifference? What if George was hiding something, something that could shed light on

Eleanor's disappearance, but which he'd deliberately buried in the past?

Felix frowned as he turned the wheel, the engine purring softly under him. He couldn't shake the feeling that George knew more than he let on. It wasn't just his manner that Felix found puzzling; it was the way George had so easily dismissed the past, as if the years of pain, the questions, the unsolved mystery had never truly mattered to him.

It was starting to look more and more like George was playing a game, perhaps without even realising it. Was he deliberately keeping things from Felix, or had he simply convinced himself that it was best to move on? Either way, the indifference seemed too calculated to be a simple coping mechanism.

Felix felt a tension building in his chest. There was too much George wasn't saying. But there was no doubt in his mind now, there was something hidden in the Blackwood family story. Something George wasn't eager to share.

He continued his journey, the car's headlights cutting through the darkening road ahead. He had to get home, to reset, to think. But he knew that once he was back in the thick of things, he wouldn't let this go. George's attitude was one piece of the puzzle, and Felix was certain it was one worth exploring further.

No, he wasn't done yet. Not by a long shot.

Felix arrived home in the early evening, the quiet of his flat wrapping around him like a blanket. His mind a whirl of thoughts and suspicions that refused to settle. He barely noticed the familiar surroundings of his home as he locked the door behind him, removed his shoes, and made his way to the bedroom.

His bed was a welcome sight. It had been a long day, filled with distractions, revelations, and moments of calm, but now that he was back, he felt it all crash down on him. He ran a hand through his hair and sighed deeply as he sank into the mattress, the cool sheets against his skin offering a small sense of comfort.

But sleep didn't come easily. As he lay there in the dark, the events of the day replayed in his mind, the conversations, the little moments, and most of all, the nagging feeling that there was something about George. Felix turned his head to the side, staring at the dim outline of the room, his thoughts spiralling back to the house, to George's words, and to the subtle unease that had begun to form around the Blackwood family story.

The more he thought about it, the more Felix was certain that he had been right to question things. There was something hidden, something George wasn't saying, and the way he had dismissed the past with such a casual air... it didn't sit right with Felix.

He closed his eyes and took a deep breath, trying to push the thoughts away, but they lingered, stubborn and persistent. The case had a hold on him again, pulling him back in like a current he couldn't escape. The answers were still out there, he could feel it in his bones.

Felix rolled over, grabbing the notebook and pen he always kept by the bedside. His fingers hovered over the page, writing down what he could remember about the day, about George's words, the way he had acted, the way the mystery of Eleanor's disappearance still hung in the air like an unresolved chord.

He had to admit it: there was more to this than he had first thought. The truth was elusive, just out of reach, and the more Felix uncovered, the more it felt like he was chasing shadows.

But that didn't mean he was going to stop. In fact, now more than ever, Felix knew he couldn't rest. Tomorrow, he would follow up on what he had learned, piece by piece. He would dig deeper into George's past, into the family's history, and into the secrets they had kept for so long.

For now, though, Felix closed his eyes, the quiet of the night filling his mind with the promise of a new day, and a new lead.

Holiday

Felix woke up to the first rays of sunlight filtering through his curtains, stretching lazily as his mind flickered between wakefulness and sleep.

As he lay there, staring at the ceiling, a single thought crystallised: he needed a break.

Not just an afternoon off, not just a quiet evening at home, he needed a proper holiday. A change of scenery, a reset. And in true Felix fashion, once the idea had taken root, there was no overthinking, no careful planning, just action.

Reaching for his phone, he pulled up a travel booking app, his fingers tapping instinctively. Where to? Somewhere vibrant, somewhere warm, somewhere completely detached from the shadows of the Blackwood case. His eyes landed on Barcelona.

Barcelona. Sun, architecture, food, and, most importantly, a complete escape.

Before he could talk himself out of it, he booked the flights, a hotel in the heart of the city, and a loose itinerary of sights to see and places to explore. He'd figure out the details later. Right now, all that mattered was that he was going.

As the confirmation email landed in his inbox, Felix sat up and exhaled. For the first time in weeks, he felt something close to excitement. He wasn't running away from the case, just hitting pause. And who knew? Maybe, just maybe, a bit of distance would help him see things more clearly.

Either way, Barcelona was calling. And Felix was more than ready to answer.

Felix wasted no time once the trip was booked. He threw open his wardrobe and started packing, haphazardly, but efficiently. A few shirts, a couple of pairs of jeans, his camera, notebook (because let's be honest, he'd never truly switch off), and a handful of other essentials. He paused for a moment, staring at his suitcase. Was he forgetting something?

Ah, yes. His passport. That might help.

Bag packed, he grabbed his phone and booked an Uber. Within minutes, he was out the door, locking up his flat and stepping onto the pavement just as the car pulled up. Sliding into the back seat, he let out a breath he hadn't realised he was holding.

As the scenery blurred past, he felt something strange, something he hadn't felt in a long time. Relief. Not being bound to an investigation, not having to chase a lead or untangle a mystery. For the first time in ages, he was just Felix, a guy off on a holiday, no agenda, no pressure.

The airport was its usual chaotic self, but Felix moved through the motions without overthinking it. Check-in. Security. A slightly overpriced coffee while waiting at the gate. The hum of chatter and rolling suitcases around him only added to the excitement.

As he finally boarded the plane and eased into his seat, he leaned back, closing his eyes. Barcelona. It was happening.

For the next few days, there would be no mysteries to solve, just good food, warm sun, and a city full of life.

As Felix sat back in his seat, the plane taxiing towards the runway, his thoughts drifted to the time he had spent with George. He hadn't expected those few days to affect him much, if anything, he had assumed he would leave with more suspicions, more questions. And while that was partially true, there was something else. A quiet lesson he hadn't quite put into words yet.

George had spoken a lot about living in the now. About not letting the past drag you into regret or the future pull you into worry. At the time, Felix had nodded along, not thinking much of it. But looking back, he realised how deeply those words had resonated with him.

He had spent so much of his life chasing the next big story, the next mystery, the next truth that he had rarely stopped to consider whether he was living his own life. His work had consumed him. Even now, this trip, was it really a holiday? Or was he just giving himself enough distance to see the case from a new angle?

Felix sighed, glancing out of the small window as the plane lifted off the ground. Maybe it didn't matter. Maybe George was right, maybe it was okay to just be for a while.

Barcelona wasn't a lead to follow, wasn't a case to solve. It was a chance to step away, to breathe, to let life happen without analysing it.

And for once, Felix decided to try.

As Felix stepped off the plane and into the warm, bustling atmosphere of Barcelona-El Prat Airport, he felt an unexpected lightness in his chest. His usual thoughts, the case, the endless speculation, the pressure to uncover the truth, seemed to have loosened just a little. Maybe George had been onto something after all.

He made his way through the terminal, collecting his suitcase and weaving through the crowd towards the exit. Just as he was about to book a taxi, he heard a voice beside him.

"First time in Barcelona?"

He turned to see a woman standing nearby, adjusting the strap of her rucksack. She had an easy confidence about her, the kind of relaxed air that suggested she was either a well-seasoned traveller or just naturally unfazed by the chaos of airports.

"Uh, yeah" Felix admitted, running a hand through his hair. "You?"

She grinned. "Nah, been here a few times. Though I still manage to get lost every time I visit."

Felix chuckled. "Well, that's reassuring."

She held out a hand. "Zara."

"Felix."

"So, Felix, what brings you to Barcelona? Work or pleasure?"

He hesitated. "Pleasure. Taking a break, you know, trying to..." He stopped himself. "Trying to just enjoy the city."

"Good choice. Though, between you and me, Barcelona has a way of pulling you into unexpected adventures."

Felix smirked. "Somehow, I don't doubt that."

Zara glanced at her phone. "You heading into the city centre? I was just about to grab a taxi, could split the fare if you're going that way."

Felix considered it for half a second before nodding. "Yeah, why not?"

And just like that, his trip had started. No investigations, no clues, just conversation, a new city, and a little spontaneity. Or at least, that was what he told himself.

As the entered the taxi, Zara glanced at him and said, "Where are you staying?"

"Icaria," Felix replied.

Zara raised an eyebrow. "No way. I'm just a few streets away."

Felix smirked. "Guess it was meant to be."

They advised the driver and started their journey to the hotels. Felix and Zara chatted easily about travel, favourite cities, and the little quirks of airports that always seemed to be the same no matter where you went. It was the kind of casual conversation that felt effortless, the kind that reminded Felix he was supposed to be on holiday, not wrapped up in his usual whirlwind of over analysis.

The taxi dropped Zara off first, and Felix watched as she slung her rucksack over her shoulder. "Maybe I'll see you around," she said, flashing a smile.

"Yeah, maybe," Felix replied, though he had a feeling their paths would cross again.

A few minutes later, he arrived at Hotel SB Icaria, stepping out into the warm Barcelona air. He checked in, dropped his bags in his room, and slid the window open wide. The city hummed below, alive and inviting.

He took a deep breath. This time, he told himself, he really was just here to relax.

After settling into his hotel, Felix freshened up and decided to head out in search of dinner. He wasn't in the mood for anything fancy, just a good meal and a relaxed atmosphere. Wandering down the streets near his hotel, he let the sounds of Barcelona guide him, the chatter of locals, the clinking of glasses, the distant hum of music.

He stopped outside a cosy-looking restaurant with outdoor seating, its warm lighting spilling onto the pavement. Just as he was about to step inside, a familiar voice called out.

"Felix? Twice in one day, starting to think you're following me."

He turned to see Zara, sitting at one of the tables, a glass of wine in front of her. She grinned, clearly amused.

Felix chuckled. "If I was, I'd be a pretty terrible detective, wasn't even looking for you."

"Well, since you're here, why not join me?" she offered, gesturing to the empty chair across from her.

Felix hesitated for only a moment before pulling out the chair and sitting down. "Alright, but if I let you pick the food and it turns out to be awful, I get full complaining rights."

Zara smirked. "Deal. But I promise you, Barcelona doesn't do bad food."

As the waiter came over, Felix realised he was enjoying himself. No pressure, no overthinking, just good company, good food, and the kind of night that reminded him why he had taken this trip in the first place.

As they ate, Zara mentioned her plans for the next day.

"I'm heading to the Sagrada Familia in the morning," she said, swirling the last of the wine in her glass. "Figured I can't come to Barcelona and not see it, right?"

Felix nodded. "Yeah, it's kind of a must-see. You into architecture?"

"Not particularly" she admitted with a laugh. "But I've heard it's incredible, and I like visiting places that make me feel small in the best way, you know? Like standing in front of something bigger than yourself, something that took lifetimes to build."

Felix thought about that for a moment. He wasn't really one for sightseeing tours, but there was something about how she described it that made him consider joining.

"Sounds like a good way to spend the day," he said.

Zara raised an eyebrow. "Are you thinking of tagging along?"

Felix smirked. "Maybe. If you promise not to give me a history lecture while we're there."

She laughed. "No promises. But if you do come, at least you'll have someone to split the ticket queue boredom with."

They finished their meal, and as they stepped out onto the warm Barcelona streets, Felix realised something, he hadn't thought about work, about cases, or even about the Blackwood mystery all evening. Maybe this holiday was exactly what he needed.

The next morning, after a leisurely breakfast at his hotel, Felix stepped outside into the fresh Barcelona air and hailed a taxi. He had arranged to pick up Zara on the way, figuring it was easier than meeting at the Sagrada Família and dealing with the crowds separately.

As the taxi pulled up outside her hotel, Zara was already waiting, sunglasses perched on her head, a bottle of water in one hand and her phone in the other. She slid into the seat beside him with a grin.

"Morning," she said, fastening her seatbelt. "Feeling ready to be awed by Gaudi's masterpiece?"

Felix smirked. "I'm feeling ready for a second coffee, but I'll settle for awe."

Zara chuckled as the taxi set off towards the famous basilica. "You really don't do much sightseeing, do you?"

"Not unless chasing a lead counts," Felix admitted.

"Well, consider this a lead into the world of actually relaxing on holiday" Zara teased. "And who knows? Maybe you'll uncover the mystery of why it's taken over a hundred years to finish building this place."

Felix leaned back in his seat, watching the city pass by. A day of sightseeing wasn't exactly his usual thing, but something about this trip, about meeting Zara, made it feel like the right way to spend his time.

An important introduction

As the taxi pulled up near the Sagrada Família, Felix found himself momentarily stunned by the sheer scale of the basilica. He had seen pictures before, but nothing quite prepared him for the sight of the towering spires, the intricate carvings, the almost otherworldly blend of organic and geometric shapes that covered every inch of the facade.

"Impressive, right?" Zara said, nudging him as they stepped out of the taxi.

Felix let out a low whistle. "Yeah..."

After weaving through the crowds and passing through security, they finally stepped inside. Felix stopped in his tracks.

It was like stepping into a dream.

Sunlight streamed through massive stained-glass windows, splashing vivid colours across the stone columns, which stretched high above like a forest turned to stone. The ceiling soared, delicate and intricate, as if it belonged to another world entirely. The entire space felt alive with light and movement.

Felix turned slowly, taking it all in. "I've been in a lot of old buildings" he murmured, almost to himself. "But nothing like this."

Zara smiled, watching his reaction. "Told you it was worth seeing."

For a moment, Felix forgot about everything, forgot about work, about mysteries, about his own tendency to chase after answers. Here, in this place, none of that seemed to matter. There was nothing to solve, nothing to question. Just something to experience.

He let himself do exactly that.

Zara and Felix wandered deeper into the basilica, their footsteps muffled by the sheer vastness of the space. Everywhere Felix looked, there was something new, columns that stretched like tree trunks into a canopy of stone and beams of coloured light dancing across the floor as the stained-glass windows refracted the morning sun.

"This place feels like it shouldn't exist" Felix murmured, still trying to wrap his head around it.

Zara grinned. "That's the magic of Gaudi. He designed it to feel like a living thing, like nature and architecture merged into one."

Felix nodded absently, his eyes following the intricate patterns above them. "Feels more like something out of a dream than a church."

They made their way towards the altar, pausing every so often to take in the details, the biblical scenes carved into the walls, the subtle shifts in light as the sun moved, the sheer sense of scale that made even the largest crowd feel small.

"Look at this" Zara said, pointing to one of the towering stained-glass windows. "It's like a fire trapped in glass."

Felix tilted his head, watching how the deep reds and oranges bled into blues and greens, the colours shifting and changing as if they were alive.

"You don't see things like this back home," he admitted.

Zara smirked. "No, grey buildings and overpriced coffee."

Felix chuckled. "Pretty much."

They continued through the basilica, taking their time, moving from one stunning detail to the next. Felix wasn't the type to be easily impressed, but there was something about this place.

As they stepped out of the basilica and back into the Barcelona sunshine, Felix stretched, taking a deep breath of the warm afternoon air.

"Well, that was something else," he said.

Zara smirked. "See? Sometimes it's good to go with the flow."

She checked her phone and then looked up at him. "I'm meeting a friend for lunch at a restaurant on top of Montjuic. You're welcome to come along if you're up for it. We can take the cable car up, it's got some of the best views in the city."

Felix considered for a moment. Part of him had been thinking about wandering off to explore on his own, but the idea of a scenic ride up the mountain, followed by a good meal, sounded better.

"Why not?" he said. "I've got nothing but time."

Zara grinned. "Great! The station's not far from here. We can catch a taxi, and trust me, the ride up is worth it."

As they made their way through the city streets, Felix let himself relax. This wasn't his usual kind of trip, just a day of seeing the sights with someone who seemed to be enjoying life.

Felix and Zara arrived at the Montjuic cable car station, where a handful of tourists and locals were already waiting. The sleek red cable cars glided in and out of the station.

Felix stepped into a cable car after Zara, and the doors slid shut with a quiet hum. A moment later, they were rising steadily above the city.

"Not bad," Felix remarked, looking out as the rooftops of Barcelona stretched beneath them.

"Just wait," Zara said, grinning. "It gets better."

As they ascended, the city unfolded before them, rows of assorted rooftops, the winding streets of the Gothic Quarter, and in the distance, the shimmering blue of the Mediterranean. The higher they climbed, the more breathtaking the view became. The Sagrada Familia, which had seemed impossibly large up close, now looked like a delicate sculpture rising from the cityscape.

"This is incredible," Felix admitted.

Zara nodded, leaning against the glass. "It's one of my favourite things to do in Barcelona. You get to see the whole city in a way you can't from the ground."

Felix found himself unusually content, watching the scenery roll by as the cable car made its way toward Montjuic.

"So, this friend of yours," he said after a moment. "Should I be worried? Secret food critic? Undercover agent?"

Zara laughed. "Nothing so dramatic. Just an old friend.

As they neared the top, the landscape shifted, and the air felt fresher. The restaurant awaited, along with what Felix suspected would be another memorable afternoon.

Felix and Zara made their way towards *El Xalet de Montjuic*, a beautiful hilltop restaurant with panoramic views over Barcelona. The terrace was already buzzing with diners, the scent of grilled seafood and freshly baked bread drifting through the air.

Lucia was already there, seated at a table near the edge of the terrace, sipping a glass of white wine. She looked up as they approached and smiled warmly.

"Zara! You made it," she said, standing to give her friend a quick hug before turning to Felix. "And you must be Felix. Any friend of Zara's is welcome."

Felix shook her hand. "Nice to meet you. Thanks for letting me crash your meal."

Lucia laughed. "The more, the merrier. Besides, with this view, even terrible company wouldn't ruin it."

Felix took a moment to appreciate it, the city spread out below, the Mediterranean glinting in the distance. He had to admit, it was spectacular.

They ordered a few tapas to share, patatas bravas, grilled prawns, Iberian ham, conversation flowed easily. Lucia was a traveller, much like Zara, and they swapped stories of places they had visited, memorable meals they had eaten, and strange encounters along the way.

"So, Felix," Lucia said at one point, swirling her wine. "What brings you to Barcelona? Business or pleasure?"

Felix hesitated for half a second before answering. "Pleasure. For once."

Lucia raised an eyebrow, sensing there was more to it, but didn't press. Instead, she clinked her glass against his. "Then here's to good food, good company, and enjoying the moment."

Felix smirked. "I'll drink to that."

As the sun cast a golden glow over the city, Felix found himself enjoying the conversation, the food, and a stunning view.

Felix took a sip of his drink, glancing at Lucia with renewed curiosity. "So, what do you do for a living?"

Lucia set her glass down and smiled. "I help solve crimes."

Felix raised an eyebrow. "You're a detective?"

"Of sorts," she said, tilting her head slightly. "I'm a psychic detective."

Felix blinked. He wasn't sure what answer he had been expecting, but it certainly wasn't that. He exchanged a quick glance with Zara, who just smirked and sipped her wine, leaving him to process the revelation on his own.

"A psychic detective?" he repeated. "You mean, like… you use visions and premonitions to crack cases?"

Lucia chuckled. "That's the general idea. Though it's not as dramatic as people think. No flashing lights or ghostly whispers. It's more like… intuition, but sharper. Sometimes I get impressions, images, feelings. Enough to point an investigation in the right direction."

Felix leaned back in his chair, considering this. As someone who prided himself on facts and evidence, he had a hard time buying into the idea of solving crimes through anything other than solid investigative work.

"And the police actually take you seriously?" he asked.

Lucia shrugged. "Some do, some don't. I don't work for them officially, but let's just say I've pointed them in the right direction enough times that a few have started listening."

Felix tapped a finger against the side of his glass. He wasn't sure whether to be sceptical or intrigued.

"So," he said, leaning in slightly, "have you ever solved a case completely on your own? No police, no help, just you and your abilities?"

Lucia smiled, a knowing glint in her eyes. "There was one," she admitted. "A missing person. Everyone thought they had drowned, but I kept seeing something different. A small town, a specific street. Eventually, I went there myself, followed the feeling... and found them alive."

Felix couldn't help but be intrigued, even if his journalistic instincts told him to remain sceptical. "And you're never wrong?"

Lucia laughed. "Oh, I'm wrong all the time. It's not an exact science." She gave him a playful look.

Felix smirked. He liked her wit. He also liked a challenge.

"Well," he said, "maybe you and I should compare notes sometime. I happen to be in the business of uncovering the truth, too."

Lucia raised her glass in a silent toast. "I'd like that."

As they continued their meal, Felix couldn't shake the feeling that meeting Lucia was more than just a casual encounter. Whether he believed in her abilities or not, one thing was certain, this trip was turning out to be far more interesting than he had planned.

Exploring

As the evening stretched on, the three of them found themselves caught up in easy conversation, the city lights shimmering below them. The atmosphere was light, the food was excellent, and Felix had to admit, this was exactly the kind of break he had needed.

At some point, Zara glanced at Lucia and then at Felix. "You know, we should do something fun tomorrow," she suggested.

Lucia raised an eyebrow. "Like what?"

"Tibidabo," Zara said with a grin. "The view from up there is supposed to be incredible."

Lucia nodded. "It is. And the amusement park is quite charming, in an old-school way."

Felix leaned back in his chair, considering it. He wasn't one for amusement parks, but he had heard of Tibidabo, the highest point in Barcelona, with stunning views of the entire city. It was also home to a historic church and an old but still-functioning funfair.

"Alright," he said, setting down his glass. "I'm in. How are we getting up there?"

"Taxi and then the funicular, of course," Zara said. "It's part of the experience."

Lucia smirked. "Unless you'd rather hike it?"

Felix chuckled. "I think I'll save my energy for the view."

With that, the plan was set. Tomorrow, they would head up to Tibidabo. A day of stunning sights, fresh air, and, if Zara had anything to say about it, probably a few rollercoasters.

Felix was waiting outside of the hotel when he spotted Zara and Lucia pulling up outside in a taxi. Zara rolled down the window and waved.

"Ready for adventure?" she called out with a grin.

Felix slid into the backseat beside Lucia, he adjusted his sunglasses and smirked. "As ready as I'll ever be."

The taxi wove through the streets of Barcelona, heading toward the base of Tibidabo. The city slowly gave way to winding roads, the buildings thinning out as they climbed higher. Felix glanced out the window, taking in the change of scenery.

"So," he said, looking at Lucia, "any psychic predictions for the day?"

Lucia smirked. "I predict you'll be both impressed and mildly terrified."

Zara laughed. "Oh, he's definitely going on at least one ride."

Felix raised an eyebrow. "I thought we were going for the view."

"Exactly," Zara said. "And what better way to see it than from the top of a rollercoaster?"

Felix sighed but smiled. He had a feeling he wasn't getting out of this one.

As the taxi neared the funicular station, the excitement in the air was undeniable. The towering structure of the Temple of the Sacred Heart stood at the summit, watching over the city. The amusement park rides peeked through the trees, adding a whimsical contrast to the historic backdrop.

"Well," Felix said as they stepped out of the taxi, "let's do this."

With that, they made their way to the funicular, ready to ascend to the top of Tibidabo.

The funicular ride up Tibidabo was smooth yet steep, pulling them higher and higher above the city. As the carriage ascended, Barcelona unfolded beneath them, a vast tapestry of rooftops, winding streets, and the shimmering blue of the Mediterranean in the distance.

Felix leaned slightly against the window, taking it all in. "Alright," he admitted, "this is impressive."

Zara grinned. "Told you."

Lucia sat back, arms crossed, a knowing smile on her lips. "And we're not even at the top yet."

The carriage slowed as they approached the summit, the grand silhouette of the Temple of the Sacred Heart coming into view. Beside it, the amusement park's old-fashioned rides stood against the sky, their bright colours contrasting with the historic surroundings.

As they stepped out onto the platform, a fresh breeze met them, carrying the scent of trees and distant food stalls. Felix took a deep breath.

Zara stretched her arms out. "Welcome to the top of Barcelona."

Felix chuckled. "Not bad. So, where to first?"

Zara and Lucia exchanged glances. "The rollercoaster," Zara said.

Lucia smirked. "Or the Ferris wheel, if you want something gentler."

Felix sighed. "I knew this was coming."

Zara nudged him playfully. "You're on holiday. Live a little."

Felix looked up at the amusement park, then at the church standing tall nearby. Somewhere between thrill-seeking and quiet reflection, they had an entire afternoon ahead of them.

"Well," he said, adjusting his jacket, "let's see what Tibidabo has in store."

Felix, Zara, and Lucia made their way up the steps, climbing toward the peak of Tibidabo. With each step, the view behind them became more breathtaking, Barcelona stretching endlessly toward the horizon.

"I can see why this place is special," Felix admitted, pausing to take it all in.

Lucia nodded. "It's one of those places that feels different when you're here. Almost like you're in two worlds at once, the city below, buzzing with life, and up here, where time seems to slow down."

Zara grinned. "And yet, you're still going on the rollercoaster."

Felix sighed dramatically. "I should have known I wouldn't get out of that."

They reached the top, where the grand Temple of the Sacred Heart loomed above them. The intricate stonework and towering statue of Christ gave the place a quiet, awe-inspiring presence. The contrast between the historic church and the playful amusement park just beyond was surreal.

"Let's take a look inside first," Lucia suggested. "Then we can let Zara drag you onto a ride."

Felix gave a mock groan but followed along, stepping into the cool, hushed interior of the basilica. The stained glass cast colourful patterns on the walls, and the flickering candles added a soft warmth to the space. For a moment, none of them spoke, caught in the tranquillity of the place.

Then Zara leaned toward Felix and whispered, "Don't think this gets you out of the rollercoaster."

Felix smirked. "Didn't think it would."

After taking a final look around the basilica, the three of them stepped back outside, blinking as the bright afternoon sun greeted them. The contrast between the serene, sacred space and the lively amusement park just beyond was almost amusing.

Zara stretched her arms. "Alright, time for some fun."

Felix sighed in mock defeat. "I knew this moment was coming."

Lucia chuckled. "You'll survive."

They made their way towards the amusement park entrance, where the sounds of laughter, distant screams from the rides, and cheerful music filled the air. Children ran past, dragging parents behind them, while groups of friends snapped photos in front of the colourful attractions.

Zara pointed toward the rollercoaster. "That's first."

Felix eyed the wooden structure warily. "That thing looks like it's been here since the 1900s."

Lucia grinned. "It probably has."

Zara grabbed his wrist and started pulling him toward the queue. "No excuses."

Felix let out a dramatic groan but followed along, secretly amused by how much Zara was enjoying this. Lucia walked beside them, looking more entertained by Felix's reluctance than anything else.

As they waited in line, the rollercoaster rumbled past overhead, shaking slightly as it sped through its course. Felix took a deep breath, watching as the next group of riders climbed into their seats.

Zara elbowed him. "Last chance to back out."

Felix smirked. "I've faced worse."

"Good," Zara said as they moved forward. "Because you're sitting at the front."

Lucia laughed. "I'm definitely sitting behind you, so I can enjoy your reaction."

Felix shook his head, stepping forward as their turn finally arrived. He had to admit, whether he wanted to or not, this trip was turning out to be one of the most unexpected and entertaining decisions he had made in a long time.

As they wandered through the amusement park after the rollercoaster, Felix turned to Lucia, curiosity finally getting the better of him.

"So, how does it actually work?" he asked. "Your investigations, I mean. The psychic side of it."

Lucia smiled knowingly. "I was wondering when you'd ask."

Felix shrugged. "I've met all kinds of investigators, but never one with, well... abilities."

Lucia nodded as they walked. "I don't sit in a dark room with candles, chanting."

Zara smirked. "Shame. That would be fun to watch."

Lucia laughed. "Maybe for you. It is more about intuition and energy. Some people call it a sixth sense, but for me, it's about noticing things, details, emotions, echoes of the past that linger in a place."

Felix raised an eyebrow. "Echoes?"

Lucia glanced at him. "Imagine a room where something tragic happened. People who don't believe in the paranormal might just feel uneasy without knowing why. But I can pick up impressions, sometimes images, emotions, even fragments of conversations. It's like tuning into a frequency most people don't hear."

Felix considered that for a moment. "So, have you ever solved a case with it?"

Lucia nodded. "A few. Not in the way you'd think though. It's never about having all the answers handed to me. It's more like getting nudges in the right direction. Sometimes I pick up something the police overlooked, a hidden object, a place someone visited before they vanished, or even a name that suddenly comes to me."

Zara leaned in. "And do the police actually take you seriously?"

Lucia sighed. "It depends. Some laugh me off. Some quietly listen but won't admit they believe in it. Others... well, I've had moments where I told them something I couldn't possibly have known, and suddenly they're paying attention."

Felix crossed his arms. "You say you have been wrong?"

Lucia smirked. "Of course. Intuition isn't perfect. But neither is traditional investigating. I don't claim to have all the answers, I just have a different way of looking for them."

Felix nodded slowly. "Interesting."

Zara grinned. "Are you actually considering hiring her?"

Felix chuckled. "Let's just say... I wouldn't mind seeing her in action."

Lucia raised an eyebrow. "Be careful what you wish for, Felix. The universe has a strange way of making things happen."

Lucia listened intently as Felix began to explain the Blackwood case, her expression shifting from amusement to curiosity. They had wandered to a quieter part of the amusement park, where the hum of the rides and chatter of visitors faded into the background.

"For me, investigative journalism isn't just a job," Felix said, leaning on the railing overlooking the city below. "It's my passion. But let's be honest, I must pay the bills. And in this case, there's a serious incentive to get to the truth."

Lucia tilted her head. "How serious?"

Felix glanced at Zara, who already knew bits and pieces of the story, before looking back at Lucia. "Five million pounds. That's the reward being held in a trust fund for anyone who can solve the mystery of Eleanor Blackwood's disappearance."

Lucia let out a low whistle. "That's not pocket change."

"No," Felix said, "which is exactly why I can't let this go. But I keep running into dead ends, false leads, people who know more than they're saying, or worse, people who think it's all a joke. The police even sent me a fake cryptic letter just to mess with me."

Lucia's eyes narrowed slightly. "Typical."

Felix turned to her. "So, what do you think? If this case is worth five million pounds, maybe it's worth your time too? We could team up, see if your intuition picks up on something I've missed."

Lucia studied him for a moment, then glanced at Zara. "And you? What do you think?"

Zara laughed. "Five million? Yeah, if I had psychic abilities, I'd at least consider it."

Lucia smirked. "I don't work for money alone, you know."

Felix nodded. "I get that. But I also know that if we crack this, it's not just about the money. It's about finally putting an old mystery to rest. The family deserves answers, even the ones who've tried to move on."

Lucia tapped her fingers against the railing, thoughtful. "Alright, Felix. You've got my attention. But if we do this, I do it my way. No dismissing what I say just because it doesn't fit neatly into traditional investigation methods."

Felix held out his hand. "Deal."

Lucia shook it. "Let's see if we can find Eleanor Blackwood, or at least what happened to her."

As the sun began its slow descent over Barcelona, the trio made their way back down from Tibidabo, catching the funicular and then a taxi towards the bustling heart of the city, Las Ramblas. The energy of the place was infectious, with street performers, artists, and the constant flow of people moving between the lively cafés and markets.

"This place is alive," Felix remarked, taking in the vibrant atmosphere.

"It's always like this," Zara said. "You can't come to Barcelona and not experience Las Ramblas."

They agreed on a restaurant with outdoor seating, the warm evening air carrying the scent of grilled seafood and spices. A waiter came over, and soon they had a table full of tapas, patatas bravas, gambas al ajillo, pan con tomate, and a pitcher of sangria.

"To new partnerships," Felix said, raising his glass.

Lucia smirked. "To solving old mysteries."

Zara clinked her glass against theirs. "And to not getting anyone killed in the process."

Felix chuckled. "That too."

As they ate, conversation drifted between light-hearted stories and more serious talk about the Blackwood case. Lucia asked Felix about what he had already uncovered, pressing for details on the inconsistencies in the reports and what he believed to be the biggest missing piece of the puzzle.

Felix leaned back in his chair. "Honestly? The biggest question is still Eleanor herself. No one really knows what happened to her. If she ran away, why? If she was taken, by who? And if she's dead..." He hesitated, then shook his head. "There's no proof of that either."

Lucia tapped her fingers against her glass. "I'll need to get a feel for things myself. Maybe there's something no one else has considered yet."

Felix studied her, intrigued. He wasn't sure whether he fully believed in her abilities, but she had a sharp mind, and he needed every advantage he could get.

Zara, meanwhile, was watching the crowd. "You know, for all the mystery-solving, we should probably enjoy our holiday too."

Felix grinned. "Agreed. We'll crack the case, but not tonight. Tonight, we eat, drink, and enjoy Barcelona."

And with that, they did.

Back to the case

As the holiday wound down, the reality of returning to everyday life crept in. Felix had spent the past few days wrapped in a rare sense of relaxation, good food, great company, and a city that had been a welcome distraction from the Blackwood case. But even as he soaked up the last bit of Barcelona's charm, his mind was already shifting back to the investigation.

On their final evening, the three of them sat at a quiet rooftop bar, watching the lights of the city twinkle below. Zara was the first to bring it up.

"So, what's next for you, Felix?" she asked, swirling the last of her drink in her glass.

Felix exhaled, leaning back in his chair. "Back to the grind, I suppose. The Blackwood case isn't going to solve itself." He turned to Lucia. "Unless you've got something pressing to attend to, are you still up for a trip to England? Could use a fresh pair of eyes on this, and if your skills are as sharp as you claim, you might help me crack this thing."

Lucia considered him for a long moment, then smirked. "I could be persuaded. Besides, I like a challenge."

Zara rolled her eyes with a smile. "You two and your mysteries."

Felix raised his glass. "To unfinished business, then."

Lucia clinked hers against his. "And to seeing what's really hiding in the shadows."

The next morning, they parted ways at the airport, Zara off to her next adventure, Felix and Lucia boarding a plane bound for answers.

As the plane soared above the clouds, Felix leaned back in his seat, turning slightly toward Lucia.

"Alright," he said, rubbing his hands together. "Let's start again from the beginning."

Lucia got comfortable, listening intently as Felix laid out what he knew about the Blackwood case. He told her about Eleanor's disappearance, the abandoned estate, and the strange flickering light that had led him there. He recounted the so-called cryptic letter that turned out to be a prank by the police, the frustrating dead ends, and how George Blackwood had retreated from public life.

Lucia listened without interrupting, occasionally nodding as she processed the information. Felix continued, explaining how he'd uncovered what seemed like a major clue, only for it to lead nowhere, and how his gut told him that something still wasn't right, something just out of reach.

"George welcomed me, treated me like an old friend, but I can't shake the feeling that he was deflecting. Not in an obvious way, but enough that I started questioning everything again," Felix admitted. "It was as if he wanted to remind me that some things are better left in the past."

Lucia tapped her fingers against the armrest thoughtfully. "And you don't believe that?"

"Not for a second," Felix said. "This case was swept under the rug. Either out of convenience or because someone wanted it to be. And I don't think George told me everything."

Lucia tilted her head slightly. "Do you think he's involved?"

Felix sighed. "Not directly. But he knows more than he's letting on. Whether that's to protect someone, himself, or just because he doesn't want the past stirred up, I don't know."

Lucia studied him for a moment, then smiled faintly. "Well, Felix, it looks like you brought the right person along. Let's see what I can uncover."

Felix smirked. "I was hoping you'd say that."

The plane hummed along, the steady sound of engines filling the air as Felix started to relax, relieved to have someone else in this with him. Whatever secrets the Blackwood case still held, he wasn't facing them alone anymore.

As they stepped off the plane and made their way through the terminal, Felix turned to Lucia.

"If you don't have anywhere lined up yet, you're welcome to stay in my spare room," he offered. "It's nothing fancy, but it'll save you the hassle of finding a place right away."

Lucia considered for a moment before nodding. "That actually sounds great. Less time searching for accommodation, more time focusing on the case."

Felix grinned. "Exactly. And I promise I won't make you pay rent, at least not until we crack this case and split that reward money."

Lucia chuckled. "Generous of you."

They collected their luggage, made their way through arrivals, and caught a taxi back to Felix's flat. As they drove through the city streets, Felix felt an odd sense of anticipation. Bringing Lucia into this wasn't just about solving the case, it was about finally having someone who might see the things he had missed. Someone who could give him a fresh perspective.

And, for the first time in a long time, he didn't feel like he was chasing leads alone.

After they unpacked, Lucia stretched her arms and glanced around Felix's flat. "Feels good to finally be here," she said, before turning her attention back to him. "So, first thing tomorrow, I think we should go straight to the estate. I need to spend some time there and see if I can pick up on anything."

Felix raised an eyebrow. "You mean... psychically?"

Lucia smirked. "That is what I do, remember?"

He nodded, rubbing his chin. "Alright. Makes sense. I've combed through that place before, but maybe you'll notice something I didn't."

"That's the idea," she said. "Sometimes, it's not about looking harder, it's about looking differently."

Felix leaned back in his chair. "Alright, we'll head out first thing. But I'm warning you now, the place is a wreck. Abandoned for years. You might want to wear sturdy shoes."

Lucia laughed.

With that, they called it a night. Tomorrow, they would step back into the mystery of the Blackwood estate.

After a quick breakfast, Felix grabbed his notebook and torch while Lucia tied her hair back and pulled on a sturdy pair of boots. "Ready?" he asked as he slung his bag over his shoulder.

"Absolutely," she said, her expression focused.

They headed out, catching a taxi towards the Blackwood estate. The drive was quiet, with Felix lost in thought and Lucia gazing out of the window, as though mentally preparing herself. The closer they got, the more Felix felt that familiar weight settle over him, the feeling that the answers were just out of reach, taunting him.

When the taxi pulled up near the rusted gates, Lucia stepped out first, taking in the decaying grandeur of the estate. "Well," she murmured, "this place certainly has a presence."

Felix paid the driver and walked up beside her. "Yeah. The kind that makes people turn around and leave."

Lucia tilted her head slightly, as if listening to something unheard. "Or the kind that keeps secrets locked inside."

Felix exhaled sharply. "Let's find out which."

With that, they made their way into the estate.

Lucia walked slowly up the overgrown path, her steps deliberate. Felix watched as she suddenly stopped, closing her eyes. She stood there, perfectly still, her breathing steady as though she was listening to something beyond his perception.

Felix crossed his arms, waiting. He had no idea what exactly she was doing, but he figured it was best not to interrupt.

Minutes passed. A breeze rustled the ivy creeping up the estate walls, and a crow cawed in the distance. Lucia's expression shifted slightly, her brow furrowed, her lips pressing into a thin line.

Finally, she exhaled and opened her eyes, looking directly at Felix.

"There's something here," she said.

Felix raised an eyebrow. "Yeah. An abandoned house."

Lucia shook her head. "No, something more. There's a weight, a lingering… sadness. A presence."

Felix frowned. "A ghost?"

Lucia gave him a small, knowing smile. "Maybe. Or maybe just an echo of something unfinished."

Felix felt a shiver run down his spine. "Alright," he said, adjusting his bag. "Then let's finish it."

Lucia nodded and took the first step towards the house, and Felix followed.

She suddenly stopped again and was silent for several minutes.

Felix felt a chill as Lucia spoke, her voice steady but distant, as if she were still half elsewhere.

"Eleanor was kidnapped," she said again, firmer this time. "She was walking when the door of a parked van suddenly slid open. She was grabbed, pulled inside before she had a chance to scream."

Felix swallowed hard. He had spent so much time chasing theories, but hearing it stated so plainly made it feel more real. "She was alive?" he asked, needing confirmation.

Lucia nodded. "Yes. She is being kept somewhere... a confined space. Small. Trapped for long periods. But she's alive."

Felix rubbed his temples. "And you said you heard trains?"

Lucia exhaled, eyes unfocused as she tried to recall the details. "Trains that pass often, probably a commuter or freight line. But then something different. A steam train. That one is rare, maybe once a month, when the tracks are quieter."

Felix's mind whirred. A steam train? That wasn't something you just ignored. There were only a handful of places where steam trains still operated on scheduled routes.

Lucia watched him for a moment, then added, "She's been waiting, Felix. She doesn't know if anyone is still looking for her."

Felix felt his stomach knot. He had chased so many false leads before, but this... this felt different. Real. He glanced back at the house, its windows dark and lifeless. Then he looked at Lucia. "We will find her."

The kidnapper

Noah moved through his morning with an eerie calm, his steps unhurried, his routine as precise as ever. The small house sat on the outskirts of town, nestled in a quiet pocket where no one paid attention to the comings and goings of their neighbours. The walls were thick, the nearest house far enough away that no one would hear anything they shouldn't. And deep inside, within a carefully concealed cavity, was the girl.

She had been there for years now. A space no larger than a cupboard, just enough for a small soft mattress fitting tightly against the walls. She could sit fully upright, her head near the ceiling, but when she lay down, sometimes the ceiling felt close enough to crush her. The walls, thick and insulated, allowed no sound in or out. The only sign that the world beyond still existed came from the insulated pipe stretching up toward the roof. A small, concealed vent drew air down into the cavity, the tiny fan inside emitting a constant, monotonous hum.

Noah had built this tiny room himself, carefully designing every aspect to ensure she couldn't be found. The door was flush against the wall, seamlessly blending in with the rest of the storage space in his bedroom. To anyone else, it was just an empty panel. To him, it was a portal to something that belonged only to him.

After brewing a cup of coffee, he sat at his small kitchen table, sipping in silence. He glanced out of the window, his eyes scanning the road out of habit. It was early still, and few people were about. A woman in running gear jogged along the sidewalk, her ponytail swaying. An old man walked his dog, the leash slack as the animal sniffed along the pavement. Noah's gaze lingered only for a second before he looked away, uninterested.

He finished his coffee, rinsed the mug, and placed it back on the drying rack with mechanical precision. Then he moved toward the bedroom, the part of his morning routine that deviated from normality. He pressed his palm flat against the false panel, feeling the almost imperceptible indent that signified the hidden mechanism. With a calculated push, the panel gave way, revealing the darkness within. A faint rustling could be heard from inside, a shift in the stale air.

He reached in and switched on the dim light, an LED strip fixed to the top of the space. It was the only illumination she ever saw. Blinking against the light, the girl curled tighter into herself, her breathing shallow and careful, as if to avoid making a sound she didn't need to. Her hair clung to her forehead, damp from the perpetual warmth of the enclosed space. Her wrists, though free now, bore the faint marks of the restraints she wore when she didn't behave. She no longer fought, at least, not in a way that mattered.

Noah crouched at the opening, his head tilted slightly as he observed her. He always took a moment to watch before he said anything. It wasn't necessary, but he liked to see how she responded. The way her body tensed just slightly, the way her fingers twitched but never fully formed into fists anymore. Fear had become ingrained into her very movements.

"Good morning," he finally said, his voice calm. Devoid of any real emotion.

She said nothing. He never expected her to.

He placed the bottle of water just inside the entrance, followed by a small portion of food, a protein bar today. Easy. Minimal mess. He preferred it that way. She took it without hesitation, fingers snatching at the bottle first. He let her have this moment, let her drink, because control wasn't about denying everything. It was about deciding when to allow.

As she ate, he reached in and ran his fingers along the edges of the cavity, checking for anything out of place. A habitual task. He had done it so many times before, but he was meticulous. Any weakness, any change in the structure, and he needed to know about it. But there was nothing. There never was.

When she finished, she retreated once more, curling in on herself, her eyes heavy-lidded. She slept often. There was little else to do when in the "hole." He liked her quiet, preferred the stillness of it. A part of him wondered what she dreamt about. If her mind had crafted an escape where her body could not.

Noah switched the light off and closed the panel, sealing her away once again. He stood, adjusting the position of the furniture to ensure everything remained exactly as it should be. Then, without hesitation, he continued his morning, moving back toward the kitchen as if nothing at all had changed.

Later that day Noah went back to the hidden space again. The house was silent. Inside the girl lay curled up, awake but unmoving. She had learned long ago that movement was unnecessary until he decided it was. Time blurred in the darkness, sometimes it felt like minutes, sometimes like hours. But when the panel slid open, she knew her body had to respond before her mind had the chance to hesitate.

Noah always stood there, watching. He always took a moment, observing as if she were nothing more than a possession, a thing to be evaluated before use.

"Come out," he said, his voice even, controlled.

She moved quickly, crawling out of the cramped space and into the open. Her limbs ached from being confined for so long, but she had learned not to complain. He hated weakness.

Noah straightened, stepping back to allow her to stand. She wavered slightly but caught herself. A mistake like that could cost her. He had made that clear before.

"You know what to do," he said.

She nodded. Cleaning. That was her task today. It was better than some of the others. She preferred the days when she was simply made to scrub the floors, wipe the dust from surfaces, or wash the dishes in the sink. On those days, he barely touched her.

She moved to the small storage cupboard where the cleaning supplies were kept, retrieving what she needed. He liked the house spotless. Everything had its place, and he expected her to understand that without being told. She did. She understood it too well.

As she worked, he remained close, his presence always there, a shadow she could never escape. He sat in the living room, reading, his eyes flicking up occasionally to watch her. She never looked back.

Her mind wandered sometimes, though she tried to keep it from doing so. She had once thought about escape and had once dared to try. It had been a mistake.

She could still feel it, the memory of the blows, the sharp crack of bone against wood as he slammed her into the floor. The bruises had taken weeks to fade, and for days afterward, he hadn't let her move from the tiny space in the wall. She had lain there, her body broken, waiting for him to open the panel again.

And when he did, she had understood. There was no escape. There was only this.

Noah set his book down with a soft thud. She tensed instinctively.

"Enough of that," he said.

She put the cloth down without question. Cleaning time was over.

Now, it was something else.

She stood still, waiting. There was no need to ask what came next. She had learned that questioning only made things worse. When he gave an order, she obeyed. When he wanted her silence, she gave it. When he needed something else, she endured.

Noah studied her, his gaze impassive, calculating. He had shaped her into this, something obedient, something that no longer fought. There was a time when she had resisted, when she had pleaded, screamed, even tried to fight him off. That time was long past.

Her body still bore the evidence of what resistance had cost her. The faint scars, the dull ache in her bones that never fully faded. He had taught her a lesson in control, and she had learned it well.

Sometimes, he spoke to her as if she were something precious, something that belonged to him in a way no one else ever could. Other times, she was nothing more than an object to him, a thing that existed for his will alone. There was no pattern, no way to predict which version of him she would face. And that was what made it worse.

The task now before her was something she dreaded, a challenge that made her stomach turn every time she thought about it. It wasn't something she could avoid, no matter how hard she tried. She had to face it, no matter how much she wished she could walk away.

Taking a slow, deep breath, she focused on calming herself. Focus on how life was, she reminded herself. The anxiety, the frustration, the discomfort, it was all there, clawing at her mind, but she knew she couldn't let it take over. She needed to distance herself from those feelings. She was paying attention to the cool air brushing against her skin. Stay in the past. Let everything else fade away.

It wasn't easy, a heavy weight she couldn't ignore. But she turned her thoughts away from it, deliberately choosing something more peaceful. She closed her eyes for a moment and visualised herself standing on a quiet beach, the sound of waves crashing against the shore, the breeze against her skin. The more vivid the image became, the further away the unpleasant task seemed. For a moment, she felt lighter, free from the burden she was carrying.

But she couldn't stay lost in that peaceful world forever. With a sigh, she opened her eyes, pulling herself back to reality. In her mind, she repeated the words like a mantra: This is nothing. Just get through it. It wasn't about pretending the task wasn't unpleasant, it was about finding a way to push through it. She had done this so many times it was not really such a big a deal anymore but not something she chose.

To shield herself from the emotional weight, she imagined herself as an observer, standing back and watching from a distance. As if someone else were dealing with the mess, and she was just there to make sure it got done. Not my problem, she thought, trying to detach emotionally. I'm just here to finish this.

With each small step, the task seemed more bearable. The pain didn't disappear, but it became easier to manage. She was now a little bit closer to the end. And when that moment came, when it was all done, the relief would be worth every second of discomfort.

There were moments when it became bearable, even oddly soothing in its own way, a strange kind of escape from everything else pressing on her mind. She focused on the rhythm of it, the repetitive motions, the routine, the quiet that came with just getting on with it. It was like a trance, where her mind could float away from the immediate weight of life and just be. For a moment, she could lose herself in the task, the act of doing something without thinking about anything else.

But it wasn't what she wanted. She pushed aside the small relief, the quiet comfort she found in the simplicity of the task. It was a distraction, nothing more. It didn't give her what she longed for, something fulfilling, something that mattered beyond the immediate. It was just a stopgap, a way to get through the present without facing the reality.

For a while, she let herself enjoy the space it created, the pause from her usual thoughts. But as the minutes ticked by, what she was postponing began to settle back into her chest. The task, in all its simplicity, was a temporary respite. It wasn't her first choice. It didn't solve anything.

Closing in

Felix had buried himself in research, combing through railway maps, old schedules, and archived records. He needed to identify locations where a standard train route ran frequently, but where a steam train also passed through at longer intervals, likely on heritage or tourist routes.

Days passed as he cross-referenced timetables, station logs, and online rail enthusiast forums. He tracked the movement of freight trains, commuter services, and special heritage rail journeys. It was slow, meticulous work, but he was used to that. The key was finding a location where these two patterns overlapped, a place where Eleanor might be held.

Several potential areas emerged, but Felix knew he had to narrow it down further. He focused on remote locations near the tracks, places where someone could be hidden away without drawing too much attention.

Felix stared at the map, his pulse quickening. The houses he found were isolated, tucked away from the main roads, with the railway running directly behind them. It was exactly the kind of place that could conceal someone for a long time without drawing suspicion.

He switched to satellite images, studying the layout. There were only a handful of houses, with large back gardens that backed right up to the railway fence. Some had sheds or outbuildings, perfect places to keep someone hidden.

Felix jotted down notes, then cross-checked property records. Some of the homes were long-time family residences, but a couple had changed hands in the last decade. One caught his attention, purchased five years ago by an anonymous buyer under a limited company. No records of renovation, no records of a proper resident.

Felix and Lucia took the trip by car to the small collection of houses. The journey was short, but the anticipation made it feel longer.

As they approached the dead-end street, Felix slowed the car, keeping his movements natural. "Let's not make it obvious we're scoping the place out," he murmured.

Lucia nodded, her eyes scanning the area. The houses were quiet, the kind of place where people kept to themselves. The railway tracks ran just behind the back gardens, hidden behind a row of trees and a worn-out wooden fence.

"There," Felix said softly, tilting his head towards one of the houses.

It was the one Felix had found in the records, the one bought five years ago by an anonymous company. It looked like it hadn't been lived in properly for a long time. The curtains were drawn, the front garden overgrown, and a battered old car sat in the driveway, its tyres looking a little too deflated to be in regular use.

"Definitely suspicious," Felix muttered.

Lucia closed her eyes for a moment, tuning into whatever instinct or ability she used. When she opened them again, her expression was serious. "There's something here. I can feel it."

Felix watched Lucia carefully as she furrowed her brow, her gaze shifting slightly beyond the house. She took a slow breath, then shook her head.

"It's close," she murmured, "but it's not this one."

Felix frowned. "What do you mean? The train line checks out, the house is barely used"

Lucia raised a hand, silencing him gently. She turned her head towards the tracks, then back towards the other houses.

"It's not this house," she said finally. "It's further down. Maybe just beyond where we can see from here."

Felix followed her gaze, eyes narrowing. The road ended just ahead, but there was a narrow gravel path leading past the last house. Beyond that, a stretch of overgrown land ran alongside the railway. It wasn't clearly visible from the main street

"You think there's something back there?" he asked.

Lucia nodded slowly. "I do."

As they drove slowly down the gravel path, the crunch of tyres over loose stones filled the quiet space between them. Past a small cluster of trees, a house came into view.

It was small and unassuming, barely visible from the main road, tucked slightly behind the thin woodland. The structure looked old but not abandoned, there were signs of life, albeit subtle. A bin near the entrance had been recently moved, and the grass around the narrow front porch was well maintained.

Felix reversed the car back a short distance away, letting the engine idle. He exchanged a glance with Lucia, who was staring at the house intently. Her breathing was steady, but Felix could tell she was picking up on something.

"This feels different," she said softly. "This... could be it."

Felix scanned the house again, his investigative instincts kicking in. If Eleanor had been held somewhere secluded, this was exactly the kind of place that fit the profile.

"Let's not jump to conclusions," he murmured, though his heart was racing.

Lucia nodded but didn't look away from the house. "I know. But I think we need to take a closer look."

Felix flipped through his notes, scanning for any mention of the owner. Sure enough, there it was, Noah Smith. The man had lived in the house for years, with no major incidents attached to his name. No criminal record, no suspicious activity.

"Been here a long time," Felix murmured, tapping the page with his pen. "Noah Smith"

Felix glanced up from his notes. The house was quiet, no sign of movement.

"Alright," Felix said, shutting the notebook. "Let's see if we can find out more about our friend Noah Smith."

As he turned the car around Felix kept an eye on the house. Nothing. No flicker of movement. Just a still, silent structure tucked away from prying eyes.

The drive back to his flat was quiet at first, both lost in thought. Felix's mind was racing, piecing together everything they knew so far. The train tracks, the steam train, the confined space Eleanor had been kept in. And now, Noah Smith, a name that meant nothing yet, but something about it nagged at him.

Lucia finally broke the silence. "He's lived there for years."

Felix nodded. "First step, dig into Noah Smith. See if he's ever come up in old reports, property records, anything unusual. If he's been sitting on a secret, I want to know what it is."

When they got back to the flat, Felix went straight to his laptop, ready to start researching.

Felix scoured every record he could think of. Property records, tax filings, utility bills, even obscure mentions in local news archives. He checked police reports for any past incidents tied to Noah Smith, dug into old business registrations, and even searched for any relatives who might be connected to him.

Nothing stood out. Noah Smith was, by all accounts, unremarkable. He had owned the house for over twenty years, had no criminal record, no major financial troubles, and nothing that suggested he was involved in anything sinister.

He rubbed his temples, staring at the screen. "There's got to be something," he muttered.

Lucia, watching over his shoulder, folded her arms.

Felix's pulse quickened as he stumbled upon another detail buried in the records, a vehicle registration. A white van, registered to Noah Smith, purchased just a few months before Eleanor had disappeared.

He leaned back in his chair, exhaling slowly. "A white van," he murmured, recalling Lucia's vision. The image of a van door opening, Eleanor being snatched inside, it might line up.

Lucia, sitting on the couch with a cup of tea, looked up. "That's it, isn't it?"

"It could be," Felix said, his mind racing. "But we need more. This proves he has a van, but not that he used it to take Eleanor."

Lucia set her cup down. "Then we need to find out what happened to it."

Felix nodded, already typing again. If Noah still had the van, it might hold the answers they were looking for.

Felix leaned back in his chair, rubbing his temples. He had spent years chasing dead ends, combing through records, following leads that fizzled into nothing. The police had investigated, private detectives had combed through every possible theory, and yet, nothing. Could it really be that Lucia, with nothing but her instincts and whatever force guided her, had led them straight to Eleanor?

It didn't make sense.

"Maybe I'm fooling myself," he muttered. "Maybe I want this to be true so badly that I'm ignoring the fact that it's impossible."

Lucia watched him carefully. "I know this is hard to believe, Felix."

Felix sighed. "But what if we're wrong? What if we're wasting time on another dead end?"

Lucia leaned forward. "Then let's find out. One way or another."

Felix drummed his fingers on the desk, staring at the house on the screen. They couldn't just knock on the door and ask if Eleanor was inside, that would be absurd. If she was there, Noah wouldn't just hand her over. They needed a plan.

"Stakeout?" Lucia suggested.

Felix nodded slowly. "Yeah. We need to see who comes and goes, what the routine is. If this is the place, then someone is keeping her there. They'll have to leave at some point."

Lucia considered this. "We also need a way to confirm if she's inside without tipping anyone off."

Felix frowned. "Thermal imaging? Maybe I can get a contact to lend me a camera."

"Or a drone," Lucia added. "Fly it close enough to get a peek through the windows."

Felix liked the sound of that. "Less risky than creeping around on foot. And if we can get a glimpse inside..."

Lucia tapped her fingers on the table. "What about sound? If she's in there, maybe we can hear something, her voice, movement, something that confirms we're not just chasing shadows."

Felix grabbed his phone. "I think I can rig something up. But first, we need to get into position and watch. See if we can get a sense of what's happening there before we make a move."

Lucia nodded. "Tonight, then?"

"Tonight," Felix agreed.

Felix eased the car into a quiet spot down the street, far enough to avoid suspicion but with a clear line of sight to the small house beyond the trees. He turned off the engine, letting the night settle around them. The occasional rumble of a passing train filled the silence, but otherwise, the area was still.

Lucia shifted in her seat, peering through a pair of small binoculars. "No movement. No lights."

Felix checked the time, it was just past eight. If anyone was inside, they weren't making themselves obvious. He reached for his notebook, jotting down the details.

"Think we're in for a long wait?" Lucia asked.

"Most likely," Felix said, rubbing his eyes. "But this is the only lead we have. If Eleanor is in there, someone has to be coming or going."

They got into the quiet routine of a stakeout, watching the house for any flicker of movement. An hour passed. Then another.

Lucia sighed, lowering the binoculars. "I don't know, Felix. Maybe we…"

A light.

A dim glow from a side window.

Felix sat up straighter. "There. Someone's inside."

Lucia lifted the binoculars again, whispering, "I see a shadow… Someone moving around."

Felix's heart pounded. They finally had something. Now they just had to figure out what to do next.

Lucia lowered the binoculars, exhaling. "Well, that's not exactly sinister," she murmured.

Felix leaned forward, watching the house intently. More lights flicked on, illuminating the downstairs rooms. From their angle, they could just make out the glow of a television screen through the window. The figure inside shifted, lounging in what looked like an armchair.

"Could just be a regular night at home for Noah Smith," Felix admitted, though he didn't sound convinced.

Lucia kept watching. "Still, if Eleanor is here, she's probably not just sitting around watching TV."

Felix drummed his fingers on the steering wheel. "If she is here, she's hidden away. Locked in a room somewhere. But where? The house isn't big."

Lucia thought for a moment. "The basement. Or an outbuilding. Somewhere we can't see from here."

Felix nodded, eyes scanning the property. "We need to get a better look without drawing attention to ourselves."

Lucia gave him a sidelong glance. "You're not seriously thinking of sneaking around?"

Felix smirked. "I'm always thinking about sneaking around. The question is whether it's a good idea."

They sat in silence for a moment, both watching the house.

"I have an idea," Felix said, rummaging through some things in the back seat. He pulled out a magazine and handed it to Lucia. The cover read: "The Watchtower - Announcing Jehovah's Kingdom."

"You knock on the front door and keep him busy with this," he continued. "Try to get inside, talk to him, and look around if you can. Meanwhile, I'll go around the back and plant a few 4G battery powered cameras I've got in the boot."

He glanced towards the house. "Hopefully, I can get them pointed at some of the windows and the exit without being too conspicuous. Once I'm done, I'll head back to the car and start it up. When you hear the engine, let him know your lift has arrived. Apologise for having to go but leave the magazine with him."

Felix met Lucia's gaze. "Whatever you do, keep him distracted until then."

Lucia stared at the magazine in her hands, then at Felix, eyebrows raised. "Jehovah's Witness? Seriously?"

Felix shrugged. "It's a classic. Nobody slams the door on you right away, and they definitely don't expect you to be snooping around while they're busy being polite."

Lucia exhaled, flipping through the pages. "This is insane."

"Insanely brilliant," Felix corrected. "Just keep him talking, ask vague spiritual questions, pretend you're on some mission of enlightenment. Meanwhile, I'll get the cameras set up. The moment you hear the car start, make your excuses and get out of there."

Lucia gave him a long look. "If I get locked inside, I'm haunting you."

Felix grinned. "Noted. Now, go spread the good word."

Lucia rolled her eyes, straightened her coat, and stepped out of the car. She took a deep breath, squared her shoulders, and marched towards the front door.

Felix, already moving towards the boot of the car, watched as she reached up and knocked.

Lucia took a steadying breath as she stepped onto the porch, gripping the magazine like a lifeline. The porch light flickered slightly, casting an uneven glow over the chipped paint of the front door. She glanced back once, Felix was already out of sight, moving swiftly around the side of the house with his cameras.

She raised her hand and knocked firmly.

A long pause. She could hear movement inside, the sound of a chair scraping against the floor, then slow, deliberate footsteps approaching.

The door creaked open just enough to reveal a man standing in the dim interior. He was older than she expected, maybe mid-fifties, with tired eyes and greying stubble. His gaze swept over her, wary but not immediately hostile.

"Yeah?" he asked, voice rough from either disuse or years of smoking.

Lucia forced a polite smile. "Good evening, Sir. Sorry to bother you at this hour. My name is Lucia, and I just wanted to share something with you" She held up the magazine, angling it slightly so he could see the cover. "Have you ever thought about finding deeper meaning in life?"

The man blinked, clearly caught off guard. His gaze flicked to the magazine, then back to her face. "Jehovah's Witnesses?"

Lucia hesitated, then gave a small nod. "Something like that. More of a spiritual discussion than anything else."

He huffed a breath, but the suspicion in his eyes eased just a fraction. "Bit late, isn't it?"

Lucia widened her eyes, feigning earnestness. "I know, and I do apologise. But I just felt a real need to stop by. Sometimes, you know, things happen for a reason."

He studied her for a moment, then exhaled through his nose. "Hmph. I suppose. Well, I guess you'd better come in, then. Bit cold to be standing in the doorway."

Lucia kept her smile in place as she stepped inside.

Meanwhile, outside, Felix was moving quickly but carefully. He crouched low as he made his way along the side of the house, avoiding the patches of gravel that might give him away. He carried three small 4G battery powered cameras. The plan was simple, position them where they had clear sightlines into the windows and exit of the property without being too obvious.

The first camera he tucked under a bush, angled slightly upward toward the living room window. Through the gap in the curtains, he caught a glimpse of Lucia stepping further inside, gesturing animatedly with the magazine. Good, she was keeping him occupied.

He crept further, finding a small wooden trellis along the side of the house. Perfect. He secured the second camera at an angle that overlooked the house and way out of the property.

The third camera was trickier. He needed a vantage point with a clear view inside without being obvious. Then he spotted an old rain barrel against the back wall. Carefully, he balanced the small device on the edge, adjusting it so it pointed toward an upstairs window.

A sudden noise made him freeze.

The back door rattled slightly, as if someone were inside, testing the handle. Felix held his breath, flattening himself against the wall. But after a few tense seconds, the sound stopped.

Inside the house, Lucia was playing her part perfectly.

She sat on a battered old armchair, still clutching the magazine as she spoke, filling the silence with an easy flow of words. The man, Noah Smith, if Felix's records were correct, leaned back in his chair, arms crossed, watching her with a mix of mild interest and impatience.

"...so, you see, in times of hardship, we look for signs, for guidance," Lucia continued, keeping her tone light. She glanced around the room, taking in the details. The place was clean, but lived in. A stack of newspapers sat on a side table. A half empty cup of coffee had long gone cold on the armrest of the chair. But nothing out of the ordinary.

Then, her eyes drifted to the hallway beyond the living room. A door was slightly ajar, leading to what looked like a staircase. Something about it made her pause. The air felt heavier there, like the space beyond that door held something hidden.

She needed to keep him talking.

"You live here alone?" she asked, feigning casual curiosity.

Noah gave her a long look before nodding. "Yeah. Been here a long time."

She tilted her head. "Must be peaceful. Though, I imagine it gets a bit lonely."

Noah grunted. "Don't mind the quiet."

Lucia took a sip of the tea he'd offered her earlier, using the moment to glance towards the clock on the wall. Felix should be done soon.

As if on cue, outside, the faint sound of an engine starting up reached her ears. Felix.

She set her cup down and gave Noah a polite smile. "Well, I really appreciate you taking the time to chat with me, but it looks like my lift is here."

Noah glanced towards the window, frowning slightly. "Already?"

Lucia nodded, standing up smoothly. "Yeah, I didn't realise how late it was. But I'll leave this with you." She handed him the magazine, making sure her fingers brushed his just enough to establish a connection. If there was any lingering energy attached to him, any trace of Eleanor's presence, she wanted to sense it.

A flicker of something. Not much, but enough to unsettle her.

Noah hesitated before taking the magazine. "Right. Well, take care, then."

Lucia nodded, making her way to the door, keeping her movements natural. The moment she stepped outside, she exhaled slowly, walking calmly towards the car. Felix was already in the driver's seat, watching.

She climbed in, shutting the door behind her. Only once they had pulled away did she let out the breath she had been holding.

"Well?" Felix asked, keeping his eyes on the road.

Lucia stared ahead, her voice quiet but firm. "She's there, Felix. I know it."

Revelations

Felix kept his hands steady on the wheel, his mind was already racing through the next steps. The cameras were in place and if they worked as planned then they would have a clearer picture of what was happening inside that house.

Lucia sat beside him, her fingers drumming lightly against her leg. She was deep in thought and her eyes were fixed on the passing landscape.

"We need to be careful," she said eventually. "This man is dangerous, and we can't just charge in without a plan."

Felix nodded. "We will continue to check the footage and if there's anything solid, let's go to the police."

Lucia glanced at him. "And if there isn't?"

Felix exhaled. "Then we keep looking."

Neither of them said it out loud but they both knew they were close, and it was closer than anyone else had ever been.

That night, Felix and Lucia didn't speak much, they both knew that there was nothing left to do not but to wait. Felix set an early alarm, but he hardly needed it, he was already awake before it went off and his mind had kept him awake long past a reasonable hour, his thoughts were circling like hungry birds of prey.

He got out of bed and brewed some coffee, he got set up at his laptop which he had on the kitchen table while Lucia rubbed the sleep from her eyes. The footage had been uploading steadily to the cloud overnight. Felix navigated to the folder where the recordings were stored.

"Here we go," he murmured. This was not the first time he had setup these cameras for surveillance activity, and he knew it was either going to be disappointing or they were going to crack this and save Eleanor.

Lucia pulled up a chair next to him and tucked her legs underneath her. She looked tense, but there was also a quiet determination in her eyes.

Felix opened the first file and skipped through the early footage of the camera setup and Lucia leaving the house. They watched the house from the different angles, and they could see some additional lights flicker on as Noah Smith moved through the rooms as he busied himself.

They continued to watch in silence as he went about his evening routine, but nothing seemed particularly alarming. It seemed like he had cooked dinner and then settled down again in front of the television, and then he occasionally stepped outside for a smoke.

"He looks normal," Lucia muttered.

"That's what worries me," Felix replied.

They continued watching and hours passed in compressed time as they skimmed through the footage, but nothing changed. The was no sign of Eleanor, and no suspicious activity, beyond the fact that an unknown man lived alone in a house with possible links to her disappearance.

Then, at around midnight, Noah did something strange, he stood by the window, looking out as if expecting someone. After a long pause, he walked out of view.

Felix switched to another camera angle and caught sight of him through an upstairs window. It seemed like he was rifling through drawers. Then just as suddenly as he had disappeared from view, he could be seen in the living room again as he sat back down to continue to watch television, as if nothing had happened.

Lucia frowned. "What was that?"

"No idea," Felix said, still watching closely. "But there's nothing strange going on so far, and no sign of Eleanor."

Lucia leaned back in her chair, letting out a breath. "Maybe she's not there."

Felix shook his head. "Or maybe we're just not seeing the full picture yet."

He sat in thought for a moment before closing the laptop. "We could sit here and watch every second of footage, or we could step away for a bit. If we don't, this is going to drive us insane."

Lucia eyed him. "You're saying we take a break?"

"Not forever" Felix said. "But just a few days. The cameras will keep rolling, and even if they get discovered, everything's backed up to the cloud. I've done this before and it's better to step away for a bit and then come back with fresh eyes."

Lucia hesitated. "And what if something happens while we're gone?"

"If something drastic happens we'll know when we check the footage. But obsessing over every second isn't going to help us."

Lucia still looked uncertain, but then she sighed and nodded. "Alright. Where are we going?"

Felix grinned. "Anywhere that isn't here."

By midday Felix and Lucia were packed and on the road. They hadn't planned a specific destination, it was just an escape. Felix was driving aimlessly at first and then suggested that they head towards the countryside. A small village he knew, it was somewhere peaceful.

A few hours later they pulled into a charming little town with cobblestone streets and flower-lined cottages. A quiet inn stood at the edge of the town square, it was the kind of quaint place that felt untouched by time.

Lucia stretched as she got out of the car and breathed in the fresh air. "I think you might be onto something, Felix. This already feels better."

They checked into the inn, a small place run by an elderly couple who welcomed them like old friends. The rooms were simple but comfortable, with wooden furniture, and large windows overlooking rolling hills.

Felix dropped his bag on the bed and exhaled. "Yeah. This'll do."

The next couple of days were unlike anything they had experienced in weeks.

Instead of sleepless nights spent staring at case files they both slept in, and instead of chasing obscure clues, they walked through market stalls and tried local dishes, drinking wine under the stars.

Lucia laughed more. Felix felt lighter.

One evening, as they sat outside with drinks in hand, Lucia glanced at him. "You know, for someone who's always tangled in mysteries, you're actually pretty good at relaxing."

Felix smirked. "Surprising, right?"

She nodded. "A little." Then her expression grew thoughtful. "Do you ever think about what you'd do if you weren't chasing stories like this?"

Felix took a sip of his drink. "Honestly? No. It's who I am. Even when I try to step away, my brain won't let me."

Lucia studied him. "Even now?"

Felix hesitated before answering. "Even now."

After four days away, they returned, and the moment Felix unlocked the door to his flat, it was time.

Lucia kicked off her shoes and dropped onto the sofa. "Let's check the footage."

Felix powered up the laptop navigating to the cloud storage, and as he clicked into the folder, he was bracing himself.

The footage had continued to upload steadily, and there was no sign of the cameras being tampered with. This was a good start.

He scrolled through the timestamps, and skipped ahead to key moments, Noah moving around the house, turning lights on and off. Nothing interesting and then he paused.

Something was different.

Lucia sat up. "What is it?"

Felix zoomed in on one of the windows. The lighting was dim but there was movement inside.

And then, finally, there was a second figure.

Felix's breath caught. It was only for a moment, a shadow moving past the frame, but it was enough. To see that someone else was in that house.

Lucia leaned in. "Is that Eleanor?"

Get help

Felix and Lucia found that their days were now revolving around analysing the footage they had captured from the hidden cameras. Every morning, they sat at Felix's dining table, coffee in hand, scanning through hours of recorded video footage. The cameras were motion activated, but they paused to take a closer look whenever something in the movement caught their eye.

They mostly only saw Noah going about his usual activities. He tended to be watching television, preparing meals, occasionally stepping out to smoke on the porch. But their real focus was on the glimpses of the young woman inside. The more they watched, the clearer it became, and they knew now that it was Eleanor.

She appeared sporadically, always in the same worn oversized clothing, with her hair unkempt, and her movements cautious. Sometimes she was cleaning, and other times, she was carrying out what seemed like small tasks under Noah's instruction. But she never stepped outside.

They watched with increasing unease, waiting for a sign of a pattern and something they could use to their advantage.

Then, after several days of reviewing the footage, they noticed something significant.

Noah left the house every Wednesday evening.

It wasn't immediately obvious at first, but after scrubbing through multiple weeks of recordings, the pattern became undeniable. Every Wednesday, just after 6:30 PM, Noah would grab his keys and leave the house. He would return between three to four hours later, they didn't know where he went.

Felix leaned back in his chair, rubbing his chin. "That's our window."

Lucia nodded with her eyes fixed on the screen. "And Eleanor never comes out while he's gone. Which means... she might be locked in somewhere."

Felix exhaled. "We need to use one of those Wednesdays to get inside."

Lucia looked at him sharply. "Break in?"

Felix nodded. "We need more proof or even better, get Eleanor out, this is our chance."

Lucia hesitated. "What if he has cameras inside too?"

Felix shook his head. "I doubt it. The way he's acting means he is too comfortable."

Lucia took a deep breath. "Okay. But we have to be careful."

Felix smirked. "That's always the plan."

But in his gut, he knew that this was the most dangerous thing they had done yet. If they got caught, there would be no talking their way out of it.

But he also knew one thing for certain, if they didn't act soon, Eleanor might never get another chance to be free.

Felix and Lucia drove slowly down the quiet street, the evening air cooling as the sun dipped lower on the horizon. The clock on the dashboard read 6:32 PM and they were right on time.

As they approached Noah's house, their hearts pounded. Just up ahead, they saw a lone figure walking towards them on the pavement.

Noah.

He was on foot, casually dressed in an old jacket and worn jeans, walking with an unhurried stride.

Lucia stiffened in the passenger seat. Felix kept his face neutral as they passed Noah, careful not to stare or do anything to draw attention to themselves.

They pulled into a discreet spot a short distance away, and just out of sight of the house. Felix cut the engine, and they sat in silence for a moment while watching in the rear-view mirror as Noah disappeared down the street, Noah didn't look back at them.

Lucia exhaled. "This is it. Our window."

Felix nodded. "No second chances. Let's go."

They got out of the car quickly but carefully, and moving with purpose, yet trying not to look suspicious. The neighbourhood was quiet, then the silence was abruptly broken as a train rumbled past.

As they approached the house Felix kept scanning the area carefully making sure no one was watching. The house itself was unremarkable being small, weathered, and uninviting. The curtains were drawn and the front door locked, but they already knew that was the case.

Felix led the way around the back, sticking to the shadows cast by the sparse trees. When they reached the back door, he knelt and retrieved a small set of lock-picking tools from his jacket pocket. He had come prepared.

Lucia kept watch, her breathing steady but tense. "Hurry," she whispered.

Felix worked quickly. He wasn't a master locksmith, but he had picked enough locks in his investigative career to handle a basic one like this, and after a few moments of careful manoeuvring, he heard the soft click of the lock disengaging.

He turned the handle slowly and pushed the door open just enough for them to slip inside.

Lucia stepped in behind him being careful to close the door quietly. "Let's find her," she whispered.

Felix nodded, his pulse hammering in his ears. They were in and now, they had to find Eleanor.

The house was eerily quiet, save for the occasional creak of the old wooden floorboards beneath their feet, Felix and Lucia moved quickly but methodically, checking every room, every corner, every possible hiding place.

The living room was small and sparsely furnished. The kitchen was even more basic with outdated appliances and an old fridge.

Felix opened a cupboard and was half-expecting to find someone crammed inside, but there was only a stack of plates and cups. Lucia ran her hands along the walls, she was pressing against them searching for any sign of a hidden compartment or a concealed door.

Nothing.

They moved down the hallway, carefully checking the bedrooms. The first was clearly Noah's, some clothes were strewn across a chair and a small bedside table had a few receipts and loose change on it. The second bedroom had a small bed, some bedside tables, a small wooden chair, a blanket neatly covered the bed. The last bedroom had a few cabinets and boxes in it.

Lucia turned back to the second bedroom in a slow circle. "This has to be it," she whispered. "This must be where she's been kept."

Felix looked around the room. His stomach twisted at the thought of someone like Eleanor was being forced to live like this, in captivity.

"But where is she?" he muttered.

They checked the bathroom. Empty. They checked the tiny laundry room. Nothing.

That left only one place, the basement.

Felix led the way down the narrow staircase with the wooden steps groaning under their weight. The basement was cold and damp, with a single flickering lightbulb casting weak yellowish light. Old rusty shelves lined the walls that were filled with old paint cans, tools, and random junk. An old workbench sat in one corner, and a few storage boxes that were stacked in another.

Lucia exhaled sharply, frustrated. "She has to be here. We've seen her on the cameras, we know she's in this house."

Felix ran a hand through his hair. "Unless there's another way in and out that we haven't found yet."

They started knocking on the walls looking for anything hollow, any sign of a hidden compartment. They even lifted the old rug on the basement floor, hoping to find a trapdoor.

Nothing.

Lucia was the first to break the silence. "Eleanor!" she called out with her voice firm but not too loud.

Felix joined in. "Eleanor! If you can hear us, we're here to help!"

But there was nothing.

No scuffling of feet. No movement. No response.

Felix looked at Lucia, frustration in his eyes. "She was here. She must be here. But either she's been moved, or we're missing something."

Lucia glanced back up the basement stairs, her mind racing. "We're running out of time."

Felix took a deep breath while running a hand over his face as he tried to think through their next move. They had done all they could on their own. They had evidence and it was enough to make a strong case but without legal authority, they were hitting a wall. If Eleanor was being held somewhere hidden in this house, they needed to act fast before Noah caught on.

"We need to change our approach," Felix said firmly. "We take what we've got, the footage, the records, and we can even tell them that we have searched the house, as wrong as that is, but we found nothing. We need to get a search warrant and help from the police. If we bring the police in, they can also question Noah and search the property more thoroughly. Eleanor is in this house somewhere, we have recorded proof. We just can't find her.

It was time to leave the house so Felix and Lucia moved quickly but carefully, knowing that any sign of their presence could tip Noah off and ruin their chances of rescuing Eleanor. They retraced their steps carefully making sure that nothing was out of place.

Felix went through the living room ensuring they hadn't left anything behind. He took a moment to glance around once more. The house had an eerie stillness to it, the air thick with the unsettling knowledge that somewhere within these walls Eleanor had been hidden away for years.

"Let's get the cameras," Felix whispered.

They stepped outside into the cool night air, ensuring that they were staying low as they moved towards the spots where Felix had set up the small battery powered surveillance cameras. The devices had done their job, capturing valuable footage but now they were a liability. If Noah spotted one, he might realise that someone had been watching him.

They worked in silence, moving quickly to retrieve each camera. Felix kept his eyes on the house, and the entrance to the property, making sure Noah hadn't returned unexpectedly. As they reached the last camera, Lucia exhaled in relief. "That's all of them."

Felix nodded, but he wasn't ready to relax just yet. "Let's go," he said, leading the way back to the car.

They moved quickly but cautiously, always keeping to the shadows as they made their way down the gravel road. When they reached the car, they climbed in and sat in silence for a moment. Felix looked through the bag making sure they had everything.

Lucia turned to him. "Do you think he'll notice anything?"

Felix shook his head. "We were careful. So, unless he's got hidden cameras of his own, he won't know we were here."

He started the engine and as they drove away, Felix finally let himself relax a little. They had done what they needed to do and now it was time to put it in the hands of the police.

The Police

The next morning Felix gathered everything they had, screenshots and selected short clips from the surveillance footage, property records, the van registration, and the timeline they had built showing Eleanor's disappearance and her likely captivity.

By the time they were ready to go Felix was gripping his phone tightly. He had reached out to a contact he had in the Police, her name was Lisa and had helped him out in the past, but she was careful what she got involved in, Felix was hoping that the evidence would convince her. He hadn't told Lisa much over the phone but just that he had something urgent and that he needed to see her in person. She had agreed to meet them at a quiet café where the meeting wouldn't draw too much attention.

As they arrived Felix spotted her immediately. Lisa sat in a booth near the back and was dressed casually with her dark hair tied back. She looked wary but that wasn't unusual because she had learned to be cautious over the years, especially when dealing with Felix's investigations.

"You said this was urgent," Lisa said as soon as they sat down. "What's going on?"

Felix slid the folder across the table. "Look at this first."

Lisa sighed but opened the folder and she scanned the documents, flipping through the notes and documents without saying a word. The more she read, the more her expression changed and went from mild scepticism to something more serious. When she reached the surveillance images, she leaned in closer.

"This is the girl you think is Eleanor Blackwood?" she asked.

Lucia nodded. "It's her. She's been hidden away for years. We saw her, but we couldn't find her when we searched the house. She's being kept somewhere inside, or there's another way in and out that we haven't found yet."

Lisa frowned, tapping a finger against the photo of Noah.

Felix leaned forward. "Lisa, we need a search order. We need the police to go in there and find her before he realises that we're onto him. If we wait too long, he could move her somewhere else and then we'll have lost our only chance."

Lisa hesitated, glancing around the café as if weighing her options. Then she sighed. "I can take this to my superior. But I'll be honest Felix, they might not act as quickly as we need them to."

Lucia spoke up, her voice firm. "She's there. We just need to get in before it's too late."

Lisa rubbed her temples, clearly thinking through the risks. Then she gave a small nod. "Alright. I'll push for it. Give me a few hours."

Felix exhaled, relieved. "Thank you, Lisa. This could be what finally brings Eleanor home."

Lisa stood. "Don't thank me yet. Let's see if we can get this order through first."

As she left the café, Felix and Lucia exchanged a glance.

Felix and Lucia remained at the café but moved to a small table near the window to have something to eat, the aroma of fresh coffee now drifting between them. The tension from their break in and the meeting with Lisa still lingered, but there was nothing more they could do for now. It was another waiting game, one that neither of them enjoyed but had played before.

Lucia absentmindedly tapped her fingers lightly against the ceramic coffee cup. "I don't like waiting," she admitted, breaking the silence.

Felix smirked slightly and pushed his plate away and then leaned back in his chair. "Tell me about it. But we've done all we can. The footage is solid, and with everything we've found, they can't ignore us."

Lucia glanced out of the window, and watched the people walk past. Life carried on as normal for everyone else, oblivious to the secret they had uncovered. "Do you think she even knows she's being looked for?" she mused.

Felix frowned. "After seven years? I don't know. She might have given up hope." He ran a hand through his hair. "But she's alive, Lucia. We know that now and that's what matters."

The waiter passed by, clearing away their plates and Felix ordered another coffee with a feeling like he would need the extra caffeine. He hated this part, it was the inaction, the waiting for someone else to take control.

"Do you think Noah suspects anything?" Lucia asked, her voice lower now.

Felix shook his head. "I don't think so. We were careful. As far as he knows, today is just another day for him. And by the time he figures out something's wrong, it'll be too late."

Lucia nodded, but her expression remained tense. "I hope you're right."

They sat in silence for a while, both lost in thought. Felix checked his phone more than once but of course there were no updates yet. The police needed time to process their request and to get the warrant approved to make their move.

"Do you ever get used to this part?" Lucia finally asked.

Felix let out a small laugh. "Not really. But I've learned that patience is the difference between making the right move and screwing everything up." He took a sip of his coffee. "We've come this far, Lucia. We'll see this through."

She sighed, finishing the last of her coffee. "Yeah. We will."

And so, they waited.

Several days had passed, each one dragging slower than the last. Felix had tried to keep himself occupied but his mind kept circling back to Eleanor and then to Noah and to that house. Lucia and Felix had done all they could but now it was out of their hands. They had no choice but to wait.

Then, finally, the phone rang.

Felix snatched it up before the second ring, his pulse spiking. "Yeah?"

Lisa's voice came through the line, calm and professional. "Felix, we've got the warrant."

He let out a slow breath while gripping the phone tighter. "And?"

"We're executing it today," she continued. "I've got a small team together and we're moving in soon."

Felix sat up straighter, his mind already racing ahead. "I want to be there."

"You know that's not going to happen," Lisa said firmly. "This is a police operation. The last thing we need is an investigative journalist lurking around, no matter how much work you put into this."

Felix pinched the bridge of his nose, frustration prickling at him. "Lisa, come on…"

"No." Her voice left no room for argument. "This isn't some undercover job you can sneak into. We have the evidence you gave us, and we'll handle it from here. You stay put."

Felix clenched his jaw, exhaling sharply. He knew she was right, but that didn't make it any easier to hear. "Fine," he muttered. "But you'll update me, right?"

Lisa sighed. "Once we're done, I'll let you know what we find. And based on the evidence, we'll be taking Noah into custody for further questioning."

Felix ran a hand through his hair with his mind jumping between all the possibilities. If Eleanor was there and if they found her then it would be over. Years of chasing clues and searching would finally yield an answer.

"Felix," Lisa's voice softened slightly, "I know this case means a lot to you. But let us do our job. If she's in there, we'll find her."

He swallowed hard. "Alright," he said reluctantly.

"Good." Lisa paused. "Stay by your phone."

The call ended, leaving Felix sitting there with his heart pounding. Lucia, who had been watching him closely from across the room slowly leaned forward.

"They're doing it?" she asked.

Felix nodded, rubbing his face. "Yeah. Today."

Lucia studied him for a moment. "You hate not being there, don't you?"

He let out a dry chuckle. "You have no idea."

She smirked slightly but then grew serious. "Do you think they'll find her?"

Felix looked down, gripping the phone in his hands. "I don't know," he admitted. "But if they don't... then we're back to square one."

Lucia nodded, understanding what that meant. They had followed every lead, uncovered hidden truths, and pieced together a puzzle no one else had been able to solve. But the real question remained, would they finally get the answer they'd been chasing?

For now, all they could do was continue to wait.

George needs to know

Felix sat in the quiet of his apartment. His phone sat on the table in front of him and the last call still fresh in his mind. Lisa and her team were executing the search warrant and soon they would know if Eleanor was truly in that house. If Noah Smith was really the man who had taken her and if this mystery that had been years in the making was about to come to an end.

His fingers tapped absently against the tabletop as his mind raced and then suddenly a thought struck him, George Blackwood needed to know.

Felix sat up straighter now chastising himself for not thinking of it sooner. This wasn't just his investigation, and it wasn't just about the years he had spent chasing the truth. George had been waiting just as long, living with the grief and uncertainty of his niece's disappearance all this time. He had abandoned his old life and left behind the estate and retreated from the public eye, but that didn't mean he had ever truly let go. If there was any chance Eleanor was still alive then George deserved to know.

Without another second of hesitation Felix grabbed his phone and scrolled through his contacts. He then hesitated for just a second as he found the number and then pressed the call button.

It rang once. Twice. And a few more times. Felix was about to hang up when a deep voice answered.

"Felix?"

Felix exhaled. "George. Yeah, it's me."

There was a pause on the other end and then George spoke again with his tone wary. "This isn't just a social call, is it?"

Felix ran a hand through his hair. "No. I've got news. Big news."

Another silence. Then, George sighed. "Go on."

Felix glanced toward Lucia who was watching him with interest as he stood up and started pacing the room. "We found something, George. You haven't met Lucia, but we've been following leads, and we think we've tracked down where Eleanor has been held all these years."

The line went so quiet that for a moment that Felix thought the call had dropped. Then George spoke, his voice barely above a whisper. "She's alive?"

"Yes" Felix admitted. "The signs point to it, and we've got surveillance footage of a girl inside the house, she looks like Eleanor, but really thin and pale. We had set up cameras and tracked movements, and now the police are moving in with a search warrant."

George exhaled sharply, and Felix could hear the emotion in his breath. "After all these years..."

Felix nodded even though George couldn't see him. "I had to let you know. I figured you'd want to be updated in real time."

George cleared his throat while regaining some of his composure. "Of course. Thank you, Felix. You know, I..." He hesitated. "I gave up hope a long time ago. But if you're right..."

Felix didn't need him to finish the sentence. "I'll keep you posted."

A pause. Then George said, "I appreciate it. More than I can say."

Felix was about to end the call when another thought struck him.

"George, there's something else," he said carefully.

"What is it?"

Felix leaned against the table, running a hand over his face. "The reward. You know, the trust that was set up to pay for information leading to Eleanor's recovery."

He didn't need to elaborate. George knew exactly what he was referring to. A substantial reward of five million pounds that had been set aside in a trust and was intended for anyone who could bring Eleanor home.

"Yes" George said, his voice unreadable.

Felix hesitated. "Look, this was never just about the money for me. You know that. I've put years into this but at the end of the day as you understand it's my job. And when I brought Lucia in, I also promised her I would share out some of the money that came from this. We both worked this case, and if it leads to Eleanor, then..."

"You don't have to explain yourself," George interrupted. "Felix, I know you and I know you wouldn't have spent this much time and this much energy just for the money. But you also did the work, and to be fair that trust was set up for a reason."

Felix let out a breath. "I just wanted to be upfront about it."

There was another pause, then George chuckled along with a low, weary sound. "You're a better man than most, Felix. Keep me updated, and we'll talk about all that when the time comes."

Felix nodded. "Yeah. Will do."

They ended the call, and Felix set the phone down, exhaling.

"How did that go?" Lucia asked.

Felix ran a hand through his hair. "Better than I expected."

Lucia smirked. "What did you expect?"

Felix shrugged. "He's been through a lot. You never know how someone's going to react when a case like this suddenly gets turned on its head."

Lucia nodded, understanding. "Well, it sounds like he appreciated the honesty. And he deserves to know what's going on."

Felix sighed, rubbing his face. "Yeah. Now we just wait for Lisa's update."

Lucia leaned back in her chair. "Think we'll hear anything tonight?"

Felix shook his head. "Doubt it. If they find something, it could take hours to process the scene. If they don't, they'll probably keep digging before giving up. Either way, I think we're in for another long wait."

Lucia crossed her arms, deep in thought. "You know, I never asked… if the trust was set up by her parents, and they're gone, who's in charge of it now?"

Felix glanced at her, impressed by the question. "George, most likely. He was left in control of the estate and any remaining family assets and I'm pretty sure he is also the one overseeing the trust."

They sat in silence for a while, each lost in their thoughts. The clock on the wall ticked steadily, marking the passage of time.

Eventually, Felix pushed himself up. "I need a drink."

Lucia smirked. "Whiskey?"

Felix snorted. "Something stronger, if I had it."

He poured himself a glass, then grabbed one for Lucia. She took it with a nod, and they clinked their glasses together in a silent toast to the unknown.

The next morning Felix was halfway through his coffee when his phone buzzed on the table. He glanced at the screen and saw Lisa's name as he grabbed the phone, his pulse now quickening. Lucia, who had been sitting across from him also immediately set down her own coffee and leaned in now sensing that this was the moment they had been waiting for.

He answered on the second ring. "Lisa?"

"We got her," Lisa said, her voice steady but filled with an undercurrent of relief. "Felix, we found Eleanor."

Felix closed his eyes for a second suddenly exhaling a breath he hadn't even realised he was holding. "You're sure?"

"One hundred percent," Lisa confirmed. "It's her."

Felix felt Lucia's hand on his arm softly grounding him. "Tell me everything."

Lisa took a deep breath. "We detained Noah last night. When we searched the house, we also brought in sniffer dogs and although it took a while they led us to a hidden compartment. It was a small, concealed room, behind a false wall. That's where we found Eleanor."

Felix felt his grip on the phone tighten. "Was she…?" He didn't even know how to phrase the question.

"She's alive," Lisa assured him. "But she's not in a good state, Felix. She's malnourished and extremely underweight. She was barely clothed when we found her and she didn't try to run or fight back, she just stood there, silent, and almost like she didn't even believe we were real. It's like… like she forgot what the outside world even was."

Felix's chest ached. Seven years. Seven years of being locked away, hidden from the world. He couldn't even begin to imagine what that had done to her.

"Where is she now?" he asked.

"We moved her to a secure recovery centre," Lisa said. "She's under medical supervision and currently receiving treatment and counselling. It's going to take time Felix. She's been in an unnatural environment for so long that reintegrating her into normal life is going to be a slow process. She barely speaks and she barely reacts to anything. It's like her mind has shut down to survive."

Felix swallowed hard.

Lisa sighed. "We've also notified George. He knows we found her, and he'll be taking custody of her when she's ready to leave the centre. But that won't be for a while because she needs time, stability, and professional help before she can even think about facing the world again."

Felix ran a hand down his face. He had spent years chasing this lead and hoping for an answer, but now that it was here it felt surreal.

Lucia, who had been listening intently, finally spoke up. "And Noah?"

Lisa's tone hardened as she heard Lucia's question. "We've got him in custody. He hasn't said much but we don't need him to talk because we've got enough evidence to charge him. We found a lot of evidence in the house that suggested that he planned to keep Eleanor hidden indefinitely. We're still going through everything.

Felix's jaw tightened. "Was it only Eleanor, was anyone else involved?"

Lisa hesitated. "We don't know yet. We're looking into possible accomplices. But so far, all evidence points to him being the one who took Eleanor, held her, and controlled every aspect of her life for the last seven years. She seems to have been the only victim we know of so far."

Felix shook his head in disbelief. "And he just let her rot away in that house all that time?"

"More or less," Lisa said grimly. "He kept her in isolation. Barely fed her enough to survive and from what little we've gathered, it seems like he had some twisted sense of ownership over her. She was never allowed outside and never had access to anything. Just four walls, silence, and complete control."

Felix clenched his fists. "I hope they lock him up forever."

"They will," Lisa said. "With what we have, there's no way he's walking free."

Felix exhaled. "Good."

Lisa's voice softened slightly. "Listen, Felix. I know you've spent years on this, and I know how much this case has consumed you. You did it. You found her."

Felix leaned back in his chair, staring at the ceiling. "Yeah. We did."

Lisa paused, then added, "You should come see her. Not yet because she's not ready for visitors but when the time is right, I think it would mean something to her to know that someone never gave up on her."

Felix nodded thoughtfully, "When she's ready."

They ended the call, and Felix sat in silence for a moment, absorbing everything.

Lucia was watching him closely. "It's done."

Felix nodded. "It's done."

She studied him. "How do you feel?"

Felix let out a long breath. "Like I should feel more relief than I do. But all I can think about is what she's been through and what comes next."

Lucia nodded. "She survived. That means she's strong and she'll recover."

Felix wasn't so sure. "I hope so."

Lucia reached across the table and squeezed his hand. "You gave her a chance and didn't give up."

Felix stared at their hands for a moment, then looked at her. "And I couldn't have done it without you."

Lucia gave a small, knowing smile. "I know."

They sat there for a while, drinking their coffee in silence, both lost in their thoughts. The case was solved. Eleanor was found and Noah was in custody.

Epilogue

Eleanor's recovery was slow but steady, with the medical team overseeing her treatment, ensuring that she received the best care possible, monitoring and helping her to improve her physical and mental wellbeing. Though her injuries were not life threatening, all the trauma she had endured had left deep scars, which were both visible and invisible. It took weeks before she could move comfortably without some pain or discomfort, and even longer before she could sleep through the night without waking in a cold sweat, with her heart racing from nightmares of captivity.

She had been strong throughout her ordeal but even strength had its limits, and now that the situation had changed there were moments when she felt overwhelmed, drowning in the memories of what had happened. But she did not have to go through it alone. George Blackwood, who was as steadfast as ever had been there when she was finally discharged from the recovery centre. He had been allowed to visit her there, and when she was released, he took her into his home, offering her a sanctuary away from prying eyes, and the relentless questions that would eventually come from the press and the public.

George's home was the perfect retreat and a place where Eleanor could breathe freely. She spent her days in quiet contemplation, reading by the window, taking slow walks, and gradually reclaiming her sense of self. The nightmares still came, but less frequently and each day she felt a little stronger.

Felix and Lucia had not been permitted to visit her while she was still in the recovery centre. The doctors had been strict about limiting external influences, ensuring that Eleanor's mental state was prioritised. But as soon as she was settled at George's house, they made the journey to see her.

When Felix and Lucia arrived, Eleanor was sitting in the conservatory, watching the rain slide down the glass panels. She looked up as they entered with a soft smile tugging at the corners of her lips.

"Thank you," she said.

Lucia moved closer and sat beside Eleanor. "How are you feeling?"

Eleanor exhaled, considering the question. "Better and getting there for sure. George has been a massive help, everyday" She glanced at George, who stood nearby with his usual composed expression. Felix smirked. "I'd expect nothing less."

Their conversation soon shifted to lighter topics, though there was an unspoken understanding that the shadows of the past few months still loomed over them. They didn't press her for details, didn't ask about the days she had spent locked away, and for that, she was grateful.

Felix leaned back in his chair. "We've all got some choices to make about what comes next?"

Lucia exchanged a glance with him. They had spent more and more time together since everything had unfolded, and it was clear that their partnership had shifted into something more than just professional collaboration. There was an ease between them now and a connection built on trust and shared experiences.

"For now," Lucia said, "I think we just take things slow. No high-stakes investigations for a while. Maybe another holiday, somewhere warm."

Felix nodded. "That actually sounds like a good idea."

Eleanor smiled, glad to see that, despite everything, life was moving forward.

Meanwhile, the man responsible for Eleanor's suffering was facing his own fate. His trial had been swift and the evidence against him overwhelming. He showed little remorse as he was sentenced with his only reaction being a bitter smirk as the judge read out the final verdict.

"Seven years," the judge declared. "The exact length of time you held Eleanor captive."

There had been murmurs in the courtroom. Some thought the sentence too light while others felt it poetic justice. But regardless of public opinion, Noah was sent to prison to serve his time.

He did not last long.

Within months, he was dead. The official report stated that he had been involved in an altercation with another inmate who was serving a sentence for murder. The details were vague, it was clear that whatever had happened, Noah had not been given the chance to fight back.

There was little sympathy for him. News of his death barely made headlines with a small paragraph buried in the middle pages of the papers. Those who had known Eleanor personally were relieved even though they did not say so aloud.

Eleanor herself had mixed feelings. When George told her the news one evening over dinner, she had simply put down her fork then taken a deep breath and nodded.

George studied her carefully. "Are you ok?"

She thought about it. "Yes. I think so."

But later that night, as she lay in bed staring at the ceiling, she felt something unexpected, it was an emptiness. Noah had taken so much from her and had stolen years of her life, and now he was gone. There was no satisfaction in it.

She turned onto her side, trying to shake the feeling. She had her life back and that was what mattered.

In the months that followed, Eleanor continued to rebuild herself. With George's encouragement, she took up new hobbies and found joy in simple things while slowly stepping back into the world.

Felix and Lucia, true to their word, took a much-needed break. They travelled, spent lazy afternoons by the sea, allowed themselves to just be. But Felix, ever the investigative journalist, could not stay away from the chase for long. Before the year was over, he had taken on another case, but one not nearly as frustrating and with less importance but still intriguing enough to keep him occupied.

Lucia who was amused by his inability to sit still joined him. "We work well together," she said one evening as they pored over documents in a small café.

Felix grinned. "I was hoping you'd say that."

www.ingramcontent.com/pod-product-compliance
Lightning Source LLC
Chambersburg PA
CBHW060354310726
48976CB00003B/816